LANTERNS FROM BLOOMSBURY SQUARE

Having completed her training at Miss Nightingale's school for nurses, Camilla Haddesley sets out for Bloomsbury Square to work for 'The Association' as a district nurse. St. Giles and its people become an important part of her life; so, too, do the tall, dark-haired Doctor James Grantly and the wealthy friend of her family, Alexander Buchanan. Camilla comes to a realization of true love, but then cholera strikes St. Giles and she makes a discovery that shocks her.

PATRICIA HEMSTOCK

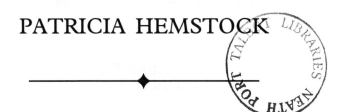

LANTERNS FROM BLOOMSBURY SQUARE

Complete and Unabridged

LINFORD
Leicester

First published in Great Britain

First Linford Edition
published 1996

British Library CIP Data

Hemstock, Patricia
    Lanterns from Bloomsbury Square.
    —Large print ed.—
    Linford romance library
    1. English fiction—20th century
    2. Large type books
    I. Title
    823.9′14 [F]

    ISBN 0–7089–7964–5

Published by
F. A. Thorpe (Publishing) Ltd.
Anstey, Leicestershire

Set by Words & Graphics Ltd.
Anstey, Leicestershire
Printed and bound in Great Britain by
T. J. Press (Padstow) Ltd., Padstow, Cornwall

This book is printed on acid-free paper

1

IN Oxford Street, Camilla Haddesley held her nutbrown umbrella firmly over her head and cursed. Another hansom had swept by, completely ignoring her outstretched hand, and splashing more mud on to her skirts. Her three-quarter brown velvet coat gave little protection to the cream swathed skirt beneath.

Around her, the people of London jostled by, hurrying poker-faced in the heavy downpour. Several times her arms had been knocked, almost pushing her on to the cobblestones of the street. On the wet pavement reflections quivered in the late afternoon light; shadows deepened under the heavy Maytime sky.

When the swirling maypoles had heralded the first of the month she had recalled her childhood with pleasant nostalgia. The Oxfordshire home, where she and her brother and sister had been brought up, had been sold just a year ago.

The village children there had delighted in their May-time dances. Yet for Camilla the memory was both bitter and sweet, for when her widowed father had died she had discovered the family fortunes to be anything but good; the sale of the house and estate had paid only her father's debts. Now, she worked, earned her own living in this great city. At twenty-three Camilla was a trained nurse.

Today she had hoped for sunshine, a good omen for beginning something new. It had, in fact, rained without ceasing. Fortunately Camilla was an optimist and would not allow mere rain to dampen her spirits. Neither, she mused, must she allow it to dampen her hat. The small round creation of cream silk was trimmed with orange and brown flowers. It tilted forward slightly, perched at the very top of her head, and held in place by a matching ribbon tied firmly under her chin. It would not do at all to arrive at her destination looking like a limp rag. She almost regretted now that she had broken her journey to do a little shopping. She needed a cab urgently, but so, it seemed, did everyone else.

Suddenly the rain quickened its pace, throwing itself at the pavement with astonishing force. Camilla glanced swiftly around before stepping beneath a brightly coloured shop awning, claiming its shelter. Only a moment, she told herself; she simply had no time to spare.

Her attention was drawn at once to a newsboy; at first she was amused. What a sight he was! Then a feeling of compassion overwhelmed her. Poor child, rain dripped from his cloth cap, the newsbill he carried was torn and soggy. How miserable he looked, moving along the street, voicing the day's tidings as he went.

"Evenin' Standard! — 'yde Park

barber 'ung for murder!"

Poor mite, he sounded completely defeated. Yet even as the thought crossed her mind, it seemed that his chin lifted a little and in his eyes she saw the glimmer of difiant courage.

Robbie Gower walked slowly on; his cry abandoned. His thin shoulders were hunched because he was cold, and because the rain kept trickling down the back of his neck which made him shudder. His trousers, thin and ragged, clung uncomfortably to his legs, making them sore. His feet were bare and dirty.

A man came towards him and hesitated.

"Paper, mister?" whispered Robbie, hopefully lifting his face, but the man turned away.

"May I have one, please?"

The voice that spoke was soft and kind. He spun around eagerly, slipping a folded paper from his bag. Then he gasped, his mouth held open in surprise.

"Cor Blimey!" he exclaimed. "I ain't never seen 'air like that afore!"

Camilla took the paper from him and opened her purse. His exclamation about her hair made her smile. Burnished copper was how she herself described the colour. She recalled with prickly anger how her mother had always insisted on calling it 'red'.

"How on earth did we beget a child with red hair?" she would sigh, patting her own black, silky locks.

Having paid the boy, Camilla was about to turn away. In the corner of her eye she had seen a hansom approaching rapidly, instead she remained motionless, staring at the boy.

"Why, I do declare you are shaking, you're quite soaked to the skin!" she exclaimed. It was all too obvious to her that the boy was ill with a fever.

"How many papers have you left?" she demanded, getting out her purse.

He watched her with wide-eyed amazement, "'bout thirty. I ain't sold 'ardly none today, Miss. They can't be bothered to stop in this bleeding rain."

Camilla counted the pennies out on to her brown leather glove then thrust them into the boy's hot hand. Uncomfortably she glanced around her before taking the papers and pushing them under her arm. "Now, home to bed just as soon as you have delivered the money."

He flashed a brief, grateful smile, then he was gone, wending his way across glassy pavements, scrambling under elbows and around damp overcoats.

Back in Oxford Street, more lights flickered on. The tempting smell of hot pies suddenly filled the air. Camilla turned on an impulse towards the pieman, but the boy was long gone.

So with the conspicuous bundle still held firmly under her arm, she tried once more to summon a cab, this time with immediate success. To her astonishment, however, she was brushed aside by a tall, top-hatted gentleman of around thirty years, who proceeded to instruct the cabman before climbing aboard himself.

"You ogre!" cried Camilla, quite overcome with emotion. "How dare you procure my cab, sir?"

"Your cab indeed, ma'am!" he exclaimed angrily. "Why, as I myself hailed it, you can scarcely lay claim to it." Then his voice softened and he shook his head. "Tell me, pray, what is your destination?"

Feeling near to tears by now, she told him she was going to Bloomsbury Square.

"Why then it is no matter," he said at once. "Permit me to offer you a ride, we pass Bloomsbury Square on our way. But do, pray, hurry. I am late for an appointment."

Which is why you so rudely commandeered my cab, she thought, but seeing it to be an argument she could not win, she gave the house number to the driver, accepted the offer of the gentleman's hand and climbed briskly beside him. Then carefully avoiding his clothes, she shook out her umbrella before laying it in the corner and settling back on to the padded leather seat. As he did not speak she decided to ignore him; he was after all an intruder in her cab. She had slipped the newspapers quickly to the floor by her feet, hoping he had not noticed them.

Already she wished she had done more for the boy. All too obviously he was in need of some expert nursing care.

"You are presumably a nurse, ma'am?" a deep voice said beside her. "I-er — recognized the address you gave."

"Yes, I am," she replied curtly, determined not to indulge in any conversation, Why, indeed she was a nurse. Had she not just completed a year at the training school of St Thomas's Hospital?

For that whole year she had planned to join The Association of District Nurses in Bloomsbury Square. Now, at last, she was on her way there, having been accepted for the three months further training before becoming a fully fledged Association District Nurse.

As the hansom jingled along, she glanced through the circular glass. All around them she saw figures hurrying, heads bent low under the heavy deluge. She was uncomfortably aware that the man beside her was watching her, but she determined to ignore him. In front of them a horse-drawn baker's cart rattled over the cobblestones, a large painted tin advertisement for NESTLÉ'S MILK on its back. On either side of them were heavily laden coster carts pulled by slow, lean-looking donkeys. In the opposite direction a brougham swept by, overtaking a horsedrawn bus with its colourful array of display plaques. HUDSON'S SOAP, OLD GOLD and RECKITT'S BLUE.

Suddenly the hansom swung left into Bloomsbury Way; within minutes the noise and clatter of the jostling carriages and carts had gone. The classic architecture of the square came into view; the only sound now was the clip-clop of the single horse, the merry jingle of the reins and the splash and splutter of the rain.

Camilla looked around her now at stately Georgian houses with their beautiful wrought-iron railings. The heavy doors were crowned by a finely patterned fanlight and elegant wooden canopy on carved brackets. Water lay in pools on the well cut grass in the centre of the square; the barks of the trees shone with wet. How nice it would be to take a walk there whenever time permitted!

The driver slowed his horse on the far side of the square. Warily she peered out, quite forgetting her unwelcome companion. There it was at last, number Twenty-Three, Bloomsbury Square, Central Home of 'The Association' which stood on the corner adjoining Bedford Place. Her eyes darted nervously from window to window of the house which was to be her home. How she had looked forward to this moment! Yet suddenly she was filled with a sense of dread. The nerves in her stomach fluttered to and fro. Really, she told herself firmly, what foolishness to have qualms at this late hour! What could there be so terrifying about it?

"If you please, Ma'am, I am late" The voice by her side reminded her swiftly of the other passenger's presence and the fact that she, too, was behind in time. Quickly she unfastened the apron door and climbed down, offering only a brief "Good Day to you, sir!" and not giving him so much as a glance.

As the hoofbeats clattered around the square she lifted her skirts and walked up the well-scrubbed steps to the front door. She had paid her own fare, of course, The gentleman had said nothing on that score, uttering only a curt "Good Day, ma'am." She sincerely hoped they would not meet again.

Moments later she followed the manservant who answered her ringing of the bell up a magnificent staircase to the drawing room. It was comfortably furnished in highly polished mahogany. The smell of beeswax and turpentine lingered faintly in the air.

The man withdrew almost immediately, saying: "I will inform Miss Lees that you are here."

So Miss Lees, the Superintendent General, was here to greet her. The lady's reputation was widespread, not only as a remarkable organizer but also as a very experienced nurse. Camilla waited, feeling nervous. Then with great dignity Miss Lees swept into the room.

"Good afternoon, Miss Haddesley," she said. "I do believe we said five o'clock. The clock in the hall has just struck fifteen minutes past."

She waited, her silence demanding an apology. Rather pale, her manner was solemn and her hair was taken back somewhat severely. Camilla was suddenly aware that her whole future might lie in this woman's grasp.

She flushed; she had expected a welcome not a reprimand on her first day. She had been used to the strict discipline of St Thomas's, but here? She knew at once that it would be just the same.

"Then I can only offer my sincere regrets, Madam. I was a little held up in town." Held up by a ragamuffin paperboy? She wanted to smile at her own lame excuse.

Her companion nodded and sat herself down on one of the Windsor chairs, indicating that Camilla should do the same. "Lateness is never tolerated by the Association," she informed her pupil firmly. "Perhaps you will remember that in future."

"Yes, indeed, madam," she answered meekly, swallowing back a curt retort. Curbing her tongue had been one of the first lessons she had had to learn. When one has been mistress of a large, country house, subservience to authority is not an easy habit to acquire.

Miss Lees explained the current working arrangements then she hesitated to look steadily at her latest probationer.

"You will find District Nursing distinctly removed from hospital nursing, but I hope you will come to like it." She then gave the briefest of smiles before rising from the chair to ring the brass handbell on the writing desk to summon the housekeeper.

Camilla was greatly looking forward to renewing her friendship with Alice Kilbride who had trained with her at St Thomas's.

On the dressing-table in her own cubicle she found a beautiful bouquet of flowers from Miss Nightingale. A little gift with which she welcomed all new probationers, Camilla was told by the housekeeper.

Alone in her new surroundings she sank gratefully down on to the bed.

Well, here she was! Bloomsbury Square at last. After a few moments of rest, however, she was soon unpacking her bags. She had faced St Thomas's and won through; then she could survive Bloomsbury Square. At least there was no opposition from her family this time. She smiled to herself; they had used all that up when she had first told them of her intention to join the nursing profession. She laughed again. Profession — that had been the boldly disputed word. After her father's death she had been faced with the choice of accepting charity from her sister's husband or earning her own living.

Her sister Bernadette was four years her junior and had married Delano Amberley, son of Sir Walter Amberley, a well known figure in financial circles, Del lived on an ample allowance, dabbling in the stock market when he had time to spare from his main occupations of riding and shooting.

Camilla laid her garments carefully in the narrow drawers and sighed. Del and

Bernadette were such children really, kind-hearted, but oh, so frivolous! Why, how truly shocked they had been when she had told them of her decision; thinking her in some kind of mental derangement. But, yes, she had known what she was doing; she had nursed her father during those long months and had had plenty of opportunity to study Miss Nightingale's pamphlets on nursing the sick poor.

She had also read her many letters to the Times. Her view was that nursing should be done by women of good general education and superior station. Camilla had allowed herself to be put into that category.

At twenty-three, she had had only one proposal of marriage and she had spent months in disgrace from her mother for not accepting it. Jago Brendon was the son of a neighbour. Not only was he ten years her senior but he had continually boasted to her of his greater experience of life. At seventeen she had no doubt, been very naïve, but she had heard enough of his reputation from the servants to know that in polite terms he would be called 'a rake'. She had turned him down quite flatly, leaving herself no time at all for consideration, and totally ignoring her mother's instructions. He was very, very offended.

When six months later her mother had died, she knew her responsibility was to take her place. Bernadette was barely fourteen and their brother Stephen sixteen. They needed her; men like Jago Brendon did not.

Now, her chances of marrying were slim; a lack of fortune reduced the odds to near impossible. She had not, however, given up hope, she professed after all to being an optimist, and anyway she enjoyed her nursing. The prospect of becoming a governess — a poorly paid childminder in her opinion, yet the only other occupation open to her — held no attraction at all.

She took out pictures of Del and Bernadette, and one of her brother who was in the army in India. She gazed at them; then the sound of a cab on the road outside brought the world of Bloomsbury back to her. Quickly she finished her unpacking, drawing back the curtain which concealed a hanging area for gowns. What she saw there made her clap her hands with delight. Hanging amidst the empty clothes hangers was the uniform of an Association Distric Nurse.

Swiftly she removed her own frock and donned the brown holland dress, then swung the dark blue cloak around her shoulders tying the matching bonnet with its edging of light blue piping. How proud she felt!

A firm knock came suddenly on the door. She called "Come in", emerging from her cubicle. When the door opened the house keeper stood there with raised eyebrows, something large and grey held firmly to her chest.

"Excuse me, ma'am," she said quickly, "but the gentleman you took the cab with said you left these. He sent the driver back with them."

Camilla stared at the bundle in dismay, then she stepped forward, her chin raised a little. The humour of the situation making her lips quiver slightly in restraint.

"It's most kind of you, Mrs Dent," she purred demurely. "I do declare I had quite forgotten them!" Then she held out her arms, taking from the bewildered housekeeper, twenty-nine copies of The Evening Standard. Then, with her most charming smile, she closed the door before leaning against it, barely able to control the ripple of laughter that shook her from head to toe . . .

★ ★ ★

In Russell Square, Dr James Grantly sank thankfully down into his comfortable leather chair with a sigh. To his left was a small mahogany table, set for tea. He leaned over and poured himself a cup, then took up a well buttered muffin and sat back to enjoy it.

It had been a trying day, one full of frustrations at how little he could do for his patients. Yet to the man who had just left a short while before, expensive medicines or treatment meant nothing. The man lived in Bloomsbury and was moderately wealthy. But St Giles! The patients there had to be content with only the sparcest of care.

It was an old subject, one that troubled him every day. He put down the tea cup he had just drained and gazed around his study trying to find something more goodhumoured on which to dwell. It was still raining outside; he could hear it beating against the window pane. From thoughts of the rain his mind wondered to his wait for a cab in Oxford Street and to the copper-haired nurse he had transported to Bloomsbury Square.

He smiled, remembering the newspapers. It had not taken much deduction to realise what she had done. He had seen the young paper boy from St

Giles often enough himself. But why, he mused, had she bought all of his papers today? Had she thought him ill, perhaps? That seemed the most likely explanation. It had rather amused him to send the papers back to her; he doubted she actually wanted them all. Yes, he would look forward to meeting the young lady again. Her striking appearance and fiery tongue had left an intriguing impression on his mind.

The door knocker clattered loudly. He listened, noting the door closing quietly in the hall. Daisy, the young maid had her day off today; Mrs Germain would answer the door. He heard her footsteps on the tiles; a man's voice apologizing then a knock on his study door.

"There's a Mr Hackett to see you, Doctor," said his housekeeper when she came in; her sleek black hair taken neatly back under her frilled lace cap.

He moved swiftly, stirred into action by the name. "Another cup, please, Mrs Germain, and I think some more muffins perhaps?"

Mrs Germain, surprised and even a little annoyed, ushered the visitor into the room. Was it really necessary for the doctor to invite his St Giles acquaintances to tea? She retreated to the kitchen without another word, throwing a brief scowl at the man.

Alfred Hackett was tall and dark-haired like the doctor, but whereas James Grantly bore his height well, Alfred Hackett stooped a little, holding his cap in front of him and occasionally wiping the rain from his face.

"Sit down, Alfred," Dr Grantly said kindly. "Mrs Germain is bringing some muffins for you; I'm sure you could manage muffins and tea?"

Alfred Hackett looked up and smiled. "Well, yes. Thank you very much, sir."

Dr Grantly settled back into his chair. "Now, why are you here?" He sat forward suddenly. "It isn't Jenny? Has the baby arrived?"

His visitor shook his head. "It's

young Robbie Gower, Doctor. Out like a light 'e is; found 'im on the pavement in Fleet Street, I did, with a crowd round 'im an all. Must 'ave been out doin' is papers. I don't rightly know what's up with him but 'e's all 'ot. Only there ain't no one to look after 'im, only 'is sisters and they're younger then 'im." He straightened his back as if to give himself confidence. "I wondered, one of them nurses . . . ?"

"Of course!" Dr Grantly got quickly to his feet and moved over to his desk where he busied himself with pen and ink. A paper boy; his mind flew at once to the copper-haired girl and he found himself seeing once more those startling blue eyes. Was his guess about the newspapers right then? It would seem very likely. Subconsciously he made a resolution to look up this boy; Robbie Gower, Alfrew had said. He didn't recognise the name but he knew the paper boy on Oxford Street by sight; if it were the same boy, he would know.

He turned towards his visitor. "Going back through Bloomsbury Square, are you, Alfred?" he asked.

Alfred nodded, then got to his feet thinking he was expected to leave.

"Sit down, man!" the doctor instructed swiftly as he crossed the room to ring the bell-pull over the mantelpiece.

Mrs Germain appeared at once with a tray. She put it down beside Alfred, being careful to not get too close to him. She would have to get Daisy to give the chair a good clean first thing in the morning. On the occasions that she herself sat down in the study that was the chair she used. She could only guess at what she might catch from a man like that.

By the time Alfred Hackett left he was less hungry and much warmer than when he had first arrived. In his pocket was the letter for the district nurses and a shilling which had been thrust into his hand for his trouble.

When the letter had been delivered safely he walked swiftly onwards until he reached the heavy door of the Dog and Gun. After being turned down for a job for the sixth time this week he decided he deserved a treat. Jingling the shilling in his pocket he slipped inside to feel the warmth of the Inn's glowing fire and enjoy the good-humoured company with a glass of ale. Jenny would do well enough with the change that was left.

When Alfred Hacket stepped once more into a cold, wet night he felt unusually cheerful. His pocket was empty now and at home, unknown to him, his fifth child, a son, had been born.

2

"WHY, is this not the man who brought the message to us about young Robbie Gower?" Miss Lees exclaimed with surprise.

Camilla looked down at the bedraggled man who lay sleeping on the wooden floor. He wore no coat and his well-worn waistcoat was neatly mended in several places. In the poor light she could just make out that his uncombed hair was dark, and on his thin face was a scar.

"Indeed it is, madam," she agreed, "but how different he looks!" She remembered the man well, especially his concern for Robbie.

She glanced around the room into which they had just walked. More light was coming in through the gaps in the slates than the small window.

She needed no prompting; already she knew the routine of a district nurse. She removed the rags from the window, revealing a broken pane of glass. At once the room became lighter; the air that came in through the broken glass was at least slightly fresher than that inside. She was surprised when she looked again for the room was much cleaner then she would have expected. Dirty, yes, but from lack of recent cleaning, not the layers of filth and rubbish they usually found.

Miss Lees was already attending to their patient who lay on a mattress of straw in the far corner of the room. She asked the four children, who sat cowering by a cupboard door, to fetch water. They darted away like frightened mice. In the grate she made a fire out of rags and twisted newspaper, and when the children returned minutes later with a pan full of water, it was put over the fire to heat.

Jenny Hackett lay very still, her eyes closed, the movement of her chest barely perceptible as she took short, rapid breaths. Her face was white and haggard from struggling alone to give birth to a still born son. Her husband seemed to have been drunk since that day. Why he had turned to drink again she did not know, nor where he had got the money from. He had needed drink once before; she had thought that time was over. Now she was past caring.

Slowly she became aware of a swishing sound like the petticoats under a swinging gown. But it couldn't be a gown. It must be Alf; her ears were playing tricks on her. She hadn't seen him all day. What hour it was, what day even, she did not know. But she had watched the dawn throw pale light across the room, and now suddenly the light was brighter, almost startling to her dry, painful eyes.

A hand touched her gently on the forehead. She opened her eyes, startled more than anything because it wasn't Alf's hand; it was soft and cool. A woman stood there, looking down at her, then she smiled and placed her fingers on to Jenny's wrist. When the woman spoke Jenny knew at once that she was a lady, and faintly, through a haze, she saw the uniform of a district nurse.

"We have come to take care of you," Miss Lees' soft voice said. "I shall wash you, and change your clothes, and put a poultice on your belly to ease the pain."

Jenny smiled, although little showed on her waxen face. She felt an uplift in her heart, a tiny spark of hope. Alf hadn't just left her to die after all, he'd fetched the nurses. Across the room Alfred Hackett slept on, unknowing.

Camilla looked across at Jenny who had had no proper attention at all since her confinement a week ago. Acute peritonitis the doctor had said; having little chance of survival. His call had been most fortunate, quite by accident it seemed.

When the children had been washed, Camilla dressed them in new clothes that some charitable organization had supplied. That done, they raced through the door and scrambled down the stairs to show their new attire to their friends.

Almost immediately the door swung open again and a young gentleman stood there, removed his black topper and let his brown eyes make a swift scan of the room before coming towards Miss Lees with a smile of satisfaction.

Camilla stared with astonishment. How strangely out of place he looked in this small room! He was tall, slim, and to Camilla his face bore the clearly chiselled outline that she considered handsome. In his hand he carried a Gladstone Bag; his profession was in no doubt. When he spoke, Camilla was not in the least surprised by the authority in his voice.

"Why I do declare, you have done it, Miss Lees!" he exclaimed warmly. "Once again you have restored my belief in miracles!" He glanced towards the woman in the bed and smiled. "I

just had to come to see for myself."
He sighed. "Indeed, after a morning
when the very daylight seemed choked
with lice and fleas, I had to prove that
salubrity could exist in these despicable
courts." He shook his head and smiled
again. "Ah, had we but a Miss Lees
around every corner!"

Miss Lees turned her head away
to hide the pinkness of her cheeks.
The doctor stepped lithely over Alfred
Hackett, and crossed to the bed where
he lifted Jenny's wrist with one hand
whilst taking out his pocket watch with
the other. As he neither put down his
hat nor bag, this required a surprising
amount of dexterity. Camilla was
impressed. Then, nodding his approval,
he laid an experienced hand on Jenny's
forehead. Yes, the wretched woman
was actually better, not recovered by
any means but now she had at least
a fighting chance of survival.

He looked back at the man on the
floor. He was glad, glad for Hackett's
sake. Damnation, he would have to

do something for the man; it was on his conscience even now. The fellow had, after all, saved his father's life out in the Crimea. Strange that they were so near in age, yet he himself had been a boy still at school when Alfred Hackett had been fighting for his country. A job, that was what he wanted, something to get him back on the straight and narrow. This drunken man that lay snoring there was not Alfred Hackett, it was a caricature, a mockery of the real man.

He bent his head down towards the woman but before he could speak, her trembling hand moved towards him, her thin fingers touched his.

"I don't feel so bad, doctor," she croaked hoarsely. "I ain't goin' to die now, am I?" Hope had given Jenny new life, just a flicker, just a halting of the draining away of her energy, but she could move, she could breathe a little easier, and now she could care.

The doctor shook his head and smiled. "Indeed, I believe you are right, madam. You are most fortunate that the angels of Bloomsbury Square have arrived once again in good time." He turned abruptly, as if to speak to Miss Lees, but in doing so, he noticed Camilla for the first time. Unlike her, however, he showed no surprise. "Ah," he said, a most devilish twinkle in his eye, "the young lady who reads a great deal!"

Camilla blushed, to her annoyance. When she had recognised him she could scarcely believe her eyes, for it was, indeed, the ungracious gentleman who had commandeered her cab; and quite transformed it seemed.

Miss Lees moved forward, a questioning look in her eyes. "You know Miss Haddesley, Dr Grantly?" she enquired.

"Oh, only briefly, ma'am, The young lady did me the service of allowing me to share her cab when I was greatly pressed for time." He glanced back at Camilla. "As she had a large amount of reading matter in her possession, I presumed her to be unusually fond of the subject." He put out his hand and took the one which Camilla offered him with some reserve. "Your servant, ma'am, Miss Haddesley, did you say?"

Camilla inclined her head, dreading for a moment that he was about to divulge the nature of the reading material to which he had referred. On the contrary, however, he said nothing, and her eyes were caught in his most disturbing gaze. She was captivated at once by those dark brown eyes into which she had not looked at all on their previous meeting. Miss Lees coughed, and immediately he released Camilla's hand and turned to the Superintendent.

"I must leave you to your good work, I fear, I have many more calls to make" At the door he hesitated, glanced once more at the sleeping man with a strange compassion in his eyes. Then, for a fleeting second he looked again at Camilla. The devil! She's beautiful, he thought, spirited, too. She actually called me an ogre! Then replacing his hat with a swift: "Your servant, ladies," he was gone, hurrying down the stairs with no concern at all it seemed, for their dangerous condition.

"A most likeable young man!" Miss Lees declared, putting on her cloak. "And most efficient," she added.

Camilla, reviewing her previous opinion was inclined to agree.

"I believe we are greatly overdue for luncheon," said Miss Lees "and I am sure we are both ready for one of Mrs Dent's excellent cups of tea."

In the narrow court outside, Camilla looked once more at the meagre houses. They had found the situation easily by the iron number disc on the wall. Once more they passed through the brick built archway on to the street and she looked back with distaste. Most of the houses had broken windows stuffed with rags or board. Slates were missing from the sagging roofs, exposing rafters which were blackened by wet. At the far end of the court was the allocation of privies, two rubble-built shacks;

intended to serve what could amount to three hundred people.

Camilla shuddered a little; the malodorous stench was quite vile; liquid sewage from the privies mixed with ash from the over-filled ash pit on the earth floor. A boy chopping firewood on one side had lifted his head in acknowledgement, women standing in doorways, many with babies in their arms had done the same. Camilla would be glad to get back to Bloomsbury that day.

The houses in the square were bathed in glorious sunlight as they retraced their wary footsteps home. Spring danced amongst the trees, uncurling young leaves, unfolding their vibrant colour on the canvas of bare, brown boughs. Scores of sparrows darted about, a thrush warbled happily above them. Standing like armies around the fresh, green grass, scores of tulips held up their cups of gold. Everywhere was the fragrance of flowers, of newly-turned soil, and the simple, clean, freshness of the air. Yet, she mused, they had walked not half a mile.

When she reached number Twenty-Three, Miss Lees banged the knocker firmly down on the door. "What a lovely day!" she exclaimed. "And those rhododendrons, are they not a truly magnificent picture?"

Camilla smiled and answered warmly. "Yes, Madam indeed they are!"

That evening, Camilla, dressed in her own clothes, left Bloomsbury Square and began walking back towards St Giles. Retracing the steps of the morning, knowing all the time that what she was doing was wrong, that Miss Lees would consider her action disobedient of the Association rules.

The golden sun of day still cast a mellow glow across the sky, but as she walked, the solid masses of buildings threw deep shadows over the quiet streets. The busy hubbub of the city had moved its core; the town shops were shuttered and silent, but all over London the tavern lights glowed brightly; theatres and music halls prepared for the movement into their midst.

In some of the houses in the square she had seen the firelight flickering on the ceilings as she passed by. Above and below stairs the grates were lit by glowing coals as children were tucked up warmly in their beds. The spring evenings were still cool, but would the children in Bloomsbury even notice it?

Soon she was leaving the tall, elegant buildings and making her way in the direction of Seven Dials. Covent Garden was silent; yet even so the echoes of the busy day with its persistent clatter and shouting, its bickering and bargaining seemed to haunt her from its bare stones.

Around her, the houses huddled together as if afraid of losing contact with each other. Shadows and coldness seemed to engulf the narrow streets. She was a little afraid. The officiality of her daytime visits had thrust all thoughts of fear from her mind; but now it came, hovering, threatening to disturb, eating away at her confidence and quickening her pulse and footsteps. She glanced around her nervously; there were so many people living in this area, so many, even now, out in the street with nowhere to go.

When she reached the house Camilla made her way along the passage to the stairs. There she lit a taper, waiting for the circle of light to spread to her feet. It was very dark in the narrow passage; the tiny glow did little more than throw pale light around her, leaving deep shadows in the still gloom. When, at last her eyes became accustomed to the light, she moved forward, cautiously climbing until at last she reached the attic. At the top she paused to brush the cobwebs from her face. How she hated cobwebs, and spiders, too, for that matter, lacing the blackness with their delicate webs.

She had first come to this house a week ago. Robbie Gower had lain quite still on his matress, so pale, so thin, yet she had recognised him at once as the young paper-boy. When he had woken and seen her there, he had been terrified, thinking that he had been put in the workhouse.

Now she was back to visit him in her own time, and as she entered the tiny room, she could see by his face, how pleased he was to see her. She had not intended to stay long but realising with shock and anger that his younger sisters and brother were still at work with their glove making in the room below she agreed to wait. Her first impulse had been to go down to give Mrs Dawson, for whom the children worked in exchange for their room, a piece of her mind.

Robbie grabbed her skirt and clung to it, pulling her back to the bed where he lay. "Don't you say nothing, Miss," he begged. "She'll bleeding well throw us out in the street if they don't do no work." His small face, pale enough after his illness, seemed drained of any colour at all. His lips trembled and his eyes were dark with terror.

With tremendous effort she composed herself. There was so much that shocked her, so much about which she wanted to speak out. She sighed. However would she manage to keep her words and actions within the bounds of her profession? Yes, it was fortunate the child had stopped her. She had no authority, of course, no right at all to interfere.

Camilla took his hand. "There's no need to be afraid!" She glanced worriedly around the room. The grate was cold and black. The sun had been warm in the daytime; a small fire now would take the evening chill off the air. There was neither kindling to light nor fuel to keep it so however. "Did the mission ladies bring you some food, Robbie?" she asked.

He nodded, his eyes lighting up, his unruly hair falling over his forehead. Impatiently he pushed it back. It had not seen a comb for a long time before

Camilla had struggled to make it tidy a week ago.

"They said they'd bring us some more tomorrow," he told her. "And d'you know what? One of 'em said the Parish is going to give us a shillin' a week an' two loaves of bread an' all!"

The light in the room was almost gone. Within minutes the pale glow in the sky sank behind the scores of blackened chimneys; only a faint cresent moon and a scattering of stars lit the sky. Camilla rose to her feet swiftly, realizing with dismay that she would have to find her way in this area of thieves and murderers with no lantern.

The sight of three young children struggling up the stairs with weariness had not cooled her temper with Mrs Dawson, nor had her memory of the earlier visit she had made to the woman's room. Six children had sat on the floor sewing, the younger ones pinned to her skirt to warn her if they fell asleep.

Now Camilla watched the same children come home exhausted. Rose Gower was eight, Joe was seven and Amy four. None of the children had ever attended school. Miss Lees' request that the school board find them places had so far been unsuccessful.

After helping the children into bed, ignoring her inclination to see they washed and undressed, Camilla tucked them in beside their brother, then crept down the stairs and out into the black St Giles's night.

Already the gas lamps were lit, but they were so far apart that between them were great, dark patches, and all along the streets were the black, gaping openings of the courts. The odour from them was less pungent in the cool, night air, but the cobbles still ran with ash and with overflow from the midden privies.

She walked quickly, restraining her desire to run; humming a cheerful hymn tune under her breath, clutching her bag tightly under her cloak. She was afraid, in truth she was terrified. The nearer she got to what she felt was safe territory, the faster her footsteps became. All around her shadows moved, dark figures came towards her in the dim light, seemed to hover before they passed her by.

From a court she heard laughter, mumbled words then a shriek of pain. She walked on, her heart thudding, perspiration forming on her smooth brow. Another court, a moan, then again louder; someone needed help, she was certain, someone in pain. She walked on. The sound of footsteps running behind her, coming nearer, nearer. She wanted to turn, to look. She walked on, steeling herself against the unknown. Her muscles were taut, her whole body bathed in an icy layer of perspiration.

It was a small boy who appeared beside her. For a brief second he glanced up at her face, then on he ran, barefoot and ragged, vanishing into the gloom. Then the street was quiet again, except for the tap, tap of her own footsteps and the loud panting of her breath.

She was almost in Oxford Street now. She saw the brighter lights, heard the welcome clatter of a horse's hooves and the jingle of the harness. A faint sound of music wafted towards her; she thought it to come from above one of the shops ahead of her and she sighed, breathing relief, almost laughing at herself. Then suddenly she was stopped. An arm that seemed to have no owner was thrust across her chest; a scornful laugh cracked close to her left ear.

She tried to scream, but heard only the bumping pulse in her head. And still in the distance she heard the faint strains of a violin playing. Then a tall, dark form loomed in front of her, obliterating all light, obscuring even its own shape. She knew only that it was a man.

She was pushed roughly against the wall, her back smarting from the violent contact with the brick. A strong arm pinned her there, held from shoulder to shoulder and thrust upwards under her throat. Again he laughed, his other hand groping inside her cloak. She plunged her purse out at him, unable to speak for the pressure against her throat. He snatched at it with another laugh and pushed it without inspection into the front of his coat.

With the pressure against her relaxed for a moment she moved in an effort to wriggle herself free. The arm came back so hard that she had to gasp for breath. Stale acholhol blasted in her face; she felt the pressing warmth of his body against hers.

"Bide yer time," he growled. "I ain't done with you yet. Pretty bit of stuff, ain't you?" His head came down towards her and his ale-drenched lips were pressed hard against hers.

Desperately she struggled. She had to get free. She had to pull herself out from his clutching grasp. His arm had been removed from her throat now.

The moment his mouth left hers she screamed again. This time she heard it, a loud piercing cry.

Swiftly his hand clapped over her mouth, but not in time. Another voice reached her ears, a loud, commanding shout, and her head began to spin so much she thought she would swoon. Desperately she fought it out, kept her balance and thankfully, her head steadied.

Her assailant turned just as a dark shape grabbed him firmly around the neck, jerking him hard away from her. At once she collected her senses and flung herself to the side. Now her heart thudded and her breath came in short, shallow bursts of relief

Her attacker began moving off, scowling at the lantern which was shone after him. With disbelief, Camilla stared; for as the lantern had flashed over his face she had seen a scar and had recognised the man instantly. It was none other than Alfred Hackett, husband of Jenny, the patient she had only left that morning.

After shouting a stern threat to the man about the police, the stranger now grabbed Camilla almost roughly by the arm. "Are you hurt?" he demanded, peering at her in the still inadequate light. He was tall, top hatted and had the voice of a gentleman.

"No, thank you, I believe I am quite unharmed," she whispered hoarsely, a little surprised to find any voice at all. She had expected him to detain her attacker but he had let him go quite free.

"Where are you going?" he asked, still gripping her arm.

"Bloomsbury Square," she replied with some reluctance, and beginning to wonder if her rescuer were any more to be trusted than the man he had rescued her from.

He stared, glanced down at her skirts as if seeing her for the first time. He voiced no amazement, just released her arm, picked up the lantern he had deposited in haste on the ground and lifted it to her face.

"Nurse Haddesley!" he exclaimed, astounded. "What the devil are you doing out here in the dark?"

Camilla said nothing; her secret was out, for in the lamp light she saw quite clearly that the man who had rescued her was Dr James Grantly. She was pleasantly surprised he even remembered her name. She was puzzled, too. Surely he must have also recognised that man, yet he had shown no sign of it.

If she had expected kindness or even sympathy from the doctor then she was disappointed. He looked for a moment into her troubled eyes, then glanced swiftly at his pocket watch.

"I have a call to make. You'd best come with me then I will accompany you home." He spoke briskly leaving her no opportunity for refusal and beginning to walk back towards St Giles.

"But I am quite recovered, thank you," she said, hurrying after him. "I really would not consider taking you out of your way, sir."

"It is not out of my way," he retorted curtly. "I live in Russell Square, you may remember. And you are certainly not safe alone around here." He glanced down at her, with a frown. Was the girl so empty-headed that she would go on alone, even now?

Camilla followed without further protest, walking silently beside him, wondering how she could defend her actions to Miss Lees, when, as he undoubtedly would, the doctor related the incident to her.

The call was brief, the patient already dead from a heart condition. There was nothing the doctor could do, so retracing their steps they walked towards Bloomsbury. For a while they were silent, although he slowed his step at intervals, realizing she was having difficulty in keeping up with his long strides.

"I trust you have learned your lesson," he said suddenly, glancing sideways at her face.

What could she do but meekly agree? His voice had been harsh; she waited for further reprimand.

It came. "I feel bound to instruct you, ma'am, that you must never again venture in that district without the protection of your uniform." His brow was lined, his mouth set firm. He turned his head and looked down at her sternly. "They hold the uniform in great respect, you know, but even in uniform you must not go there in the hours of darkness unless instructed to do so by Miss Lees."

"Indeed I will not, Dr Grantly. I am most unlikely to forget."

"You had returned to see one of your patients, no doubt?"

"Yes."

"A mistake, I fear, always a mistake." He sighed and for the first time she heard a note of sympathy in his tone. "We can but do our own work as well as we are able. There are various organizations to deal with other aspects of the problem." He glanced down at her again one eyebrow raised in question. "For instance, small boys with sisters and a brother to support?"

He even knew where she had been, yet surely it must only be a guess? She wondered suddenly if he had made any connection between Robbie and the newspapers she had been carrying. She had a growing desire to get to know this man better.

"Those organizations do not appear to deal very well with their side of the problems," she suggested warily.

He sighed. "Alas Miss Haddesley — " he replied with a touch of bitterness in his voice — "there I must agree with you. But unfortunately we cannot do it all."

He swung the lantern slightly and she looked up and saw a smile curving his lips. "Ah, here we are!" he said. "A place you will no doubt have pleasure in seeing tonight." He wondered suddenly if she had recognised Hackett, Gad, he hoped not! The fellow was an idiot turning to drink like that. And such a straight, hardworking young man he had been before.

They had reached the square; he did not turn the corner, however, but stopped in the shadows on Bloomsbury Way. Here, he held up the lantern, carefully shining it around her, making a thorough inspection of her person.

"There appears little amiss to the eye," he observed at last. "Ah . . . except . . . " He moved forward, lifting her hat a little and pushing away some stray hairs before straightening the hat very gently.

She began to thank him, quite astonished by his action but he just grunted inaudibly and began walking again until they reached number Twenty-Three.

"I shall not inform Miss Lees of your foolishness on this occasion — " he told her — "but I trust that in future you will obey the rules." There was not a sign of a smile on his lips now, not a glimmer of the humour that she had seen that morning in those dark, brown eyes. He raised his hat; bowed graciously. "I bid you a very good night, Miss Haddesley." Then a twinkle, just the glimmer of a twinkle in his eye. "I trust you enjoyed the concert which you attended this evening." And before she could reply, he was gone, striding briskly around the corner and down Bedford Place.

How pompous of him, how abominably pompous! She rang the bell, nearly bursting with indignation, quite forgetting for the moment that less than half an hour before she had had her bag stolen and had nearly been ravished by Mr Alfred Hackett.

Yet suddenly she remembered his last remark, a musical concert he had suggested, surely intended as an alibi, should she be questioned about her evening's activities. For the rest of that evening she found her thoughts returning again and again to those deep brown eyes.

What was he really? Pompous, kind, self-opionated, generous? Something in her longed to find out. Some part deep inside her found him astonishingly attractive, despite the apparent severity of his words and the occasional abruptness of his manner.

3

THE sunlight danced through the trees as Camilla walked down the steps of St George's Church. She wore her best blue silk dress with a pleated overskirt and waterfall back. Her matching hat was decorated by tiny white flowers. By her side was her close friend, Alice Kilbride, who was dressed in pale mauve.

"Miss Lees is having a most amicable discussion with the Reverend Craven!" Alice observed of their Superintendent.

Camilla cast a swift glance behind as they turned out on to the causeway. "I believe he is involved with the Association," she reminded Alice. "I wonder, should we wait for her?" She smiled suddenly. "They are of course, of a similar age and both unmarried."

Alice was prevented from replying by another voice quite close behind them.

"Your pardon, ladies, but may I beg a moment of your time?"

They turned almost together, recognising the voice of a certain doctor who was quite a regular topic of discussion at their Bloomsbury Square house.

Alice was the first to speak. "Good morning, Dr Grantly!" She allowed a smile for the lady by his side but wondered who she was. The dress she wore was a somewhat sombre, dark grey, but her deep-set, black eyes and thick black hair were quite startling. The lady inclined her head only slightly, retaining an air of dignity.

Camilla, being now a little behind her friend, greeted the doctor but did not see his companion at first.

"May I introduce my housekeeper, Mrs Germain?" he said, looking directly at Camilla. "Mrs Germain, this is Miss Haddesley." They acknowledged each other with a brief nod. "And Miss Kilbride?"

Camilla was a little surprised that he had interrupted their departure to introduce a mere housekeeper. She found herself wondering how old the lady was. Rather older than she was herself, she thought. There was a clarity, an aliveness in those black eyes, and an air of superiority about her as if she would like to put Alice and her down. Camilla found herself instinctively disliking Mrs Germain.

She looked up at Dr Grantly, remembering the occasion when he had rescued her from the attentions of Alfred Hackett. He had never mentioned it since. The recollection brought a pinkness to her cheeks; and she had to look away to avoid meeting his brown eyes.

The doctor thrust his hand in his pocket and took out an envelope.

"It is indeed fortunate that we met today, Miss Haddesley, for I had completely forgotten this letter."

He handed it over to her; she looked at it with surprise. Mrs Germain was visibly irritated.

"A common mistake — " he went

on — "the postboy mistook the squares. The number of my house is also twenty-three. Do pray open it this instant, and if it requires an urgent reply, then I insist it be sent at my expense, for I have carried it around with me since yesterday."

Having no paper knife at hand Camilla took out her scissors and slit open the envelope. A quick glance through the pages told her that nothing was amiss.

"From my sister, Dr Grantly, just to tell me they are come to their London house, and that I should visit them. My sister is married to Mr Delano Amberly, son of Sir Walter; you may know the family perhaps?" She lifted her eyebrows in question, aware at once of his interest and aware also of a disapproving stare from his companion.

He smiled, a lopsided smile that sent her heart racing unbearably. "Ah yes — " His brown brown eyes flickered over her face. "I know of the family, of course,"

Camilla smiled, well satisfied that the opportunity had arisen for her to tell him how well connected she was. It wasn't a ploy she used very often, in fact, she was a little surprised at herself. Out of the corner of her eye she noticed that Mrs Germain's erect frame seemed to sag slightly. Could the woman possibly have designs on Dr Grantly herself? Surely not! The idea was rather amusing.

Suddenly Camilla was fired to play the game herself; why, after all, should she not contrive to find a husband? Dr Grantly seemed the perfect victim for such a plan, and indeed she was conscious of a growing liking for the man. Yes, she would give Mrs Germain some competition at this game. What foolishness, she chided herself, but what a challenge!

When they parted there were little hard lines on the housekeeper's face. Her smile, as they bade the nurses goodbye held no softness in its curve. To her this meeting was like a warning bell. That smile, that tone in his voice a carillon crying 'beware'! Nothing must come in her way now.

All these months since she had been widowed by an old man and left nothing of his great wealth, she had planned to get and keep this post, and to keep James Grantly for herself. When he had first offered her a home the hope had grown into fervent desire. She thought she loved him, but it was a jealous, possessive love. Never had she loved before, not as a woman nor as a child. She knew he would never marry her, yet she saw herself as becoming an indispensable part of his life, Mistress of his small but comfortable household. Not a great catch, she knew, but with no money or position of her own, she saw nothing better on the horizon. So she would take it, yes take, pushing aside any obstacle in the way.

Now, suddenly, this Miss Haddesley had become an obstacle; one she must deal with before it was too late. As a woman she was aware of her one virtue, her looks. As a girl she had been more than pretty, she had been lovely; black curls framing her pale, clear skin; her slim curved figure only adding pleasure to the eye. Now, as a mature woman she was still able to be proud of her body. James Grantly had noticed her looks, she knew that. She was also a good housekeeper. She had made sure he noticed that, too.

But suddenly Miss Haddesley had entered the scene and Mrs Germain saw her only as an object of hatred. The nurse had youth on her side and that lovely red hair. There was only one course open; she must be destroyed . . .

★ ★ ★

"Camilla, why, Camilla darling, how absolutely gorgeous to see you!" Bernadette Amberley, slim and black-haired, almost leapt across the room towards her sister.

Camilla smiled. "You look wonderful,

my dear," she assured Bernadette quite candidly "You are happy, too, I can see that you are happy."

A swift colour rose to Bernadette's cheeks; her eyes, blue like Camillla's dropped instantly to the floor. Then she laughed shortly and was herself again, scolding her sister for not coming earlier in the day, leading her by the hand to the crimson, velvet covered sofa by the blazing fire.

Camilla let her gaze wander around the enormous drawing room. It had not changed. Heavily furnished, the deep rose coloured flowers of the carpet were reflected not only in the wall paper but also by the ornate carvings on the chair and table legs. All of the pieces in this room were in themselves valuable; their compatibility was less obvious. An absurd profusion of ornaments cluttered every horizontal surface.

Camilla had never liked this room. In a strange way she compared it with the fairy-like elegance of her old home, but then she hadn't really liked that either.

Something simpler, more clear cut with beautifully blending colours was more to her taste.

Bernadette caught her somewhat critical eye as it scanned the room. "You will never guess who is to dine with us tomorrow evening," she exclaimed with childlike excitement. "Mr Morris, Mr William Morris!"

Camilla had, of course, heard of the gentleman but had seen very little of his work. She tried to look interested.

"He is coming to advise us on decoration." Bernadette clasped her hands together tightly, her eyes darting from wall to wall. "We shall start in here. Del says I may change anything I wish, new furniture, new carpets. Will it not be thrilling to have a William Morris room?" She looked back towards Camilla earnestly. "Do you know what Mr Morris says, Camilla?"

Camilla shook her head, laughing. She had not the slightest notion.

"He says: Have nothing in your

house that you do not know to be useful or believe to be beautiful." She touched her sister's arm affectionately. "Do you not agree that is wonderful? Lady Lowering has had her whole house done according to Mr Morris's instructions. Del and I were gloriously impressed!"

Camilla smiled and nodded. There seemed little she could say. The room could certainly do with some changes; it would undoubtedly be improved. But in her mind she saw another room, a small bare room with certainly nothing whatsoever in it that was not useful, but nothing either that was beautiful. Robbie Gower's room had little furniture at all, yet Bernadette could change all of hers for a mere whim of fashion.

"I am greatly vexed with you," Bernadette announced suddenly, trying to sound stern, but her eyes betraying laughter. "We expected a visit from you two days ago. Why, you missed the Richmond!"

Camilla shook her head, smiling. "But, Bernadette, I have to work," she reminded her firmly. "I cannot just take off my uniform and leave when I please. I have come at the first opportunity and you must be satisfied with that." She sighed deeply, allowing herself to reminisce for a moment. "There are many things I shall miss in London this season. You know how I love to see the Shires at the Richmond, but I have made my choice and now my work is more important."

Bernadette looked shocked; laid her delicate hands on her applegreen gown, smoothing the silk with her fingers. "But, Camilla, you will surely take a holiday whilst we are in town. I am counting on you to come to Ascot with us."

Camilla laughed a little ruefully, shaking her head again. How well she remembered Ascot. The bright blue four-in-hand in which she had travelled on her last visit there, the exquisite dresses and glorious hats . . . but no, she would not be at Ascot this year.

It was not easy to convince Bernadette that one did not simply request a holiday from Miss Lees. Last season her annual holiday had coincided with Del and Bernadette's stay in London. "There will be a few days off in August — " she explained with as much patience as she could muster — "but until then I must work every day."

Bernadette burst into tears; there was no way of holding back her acute disappointment.

Camilla tried to console her. "We shall have heaps and heaps to talk about when I do come, my darling, and you shall tell me all about the places you visit."

"Then you will at least stay for this evening," Bernadette said at last, after blowing her nose and forcing a smile through the tears. "It is only a drum; you will know all of our guests. Please say you will stay, Camilla or I will be most dreadfully disappointed."

Camilla glanced down at her brown brocade. "I am scarcely attired for entertaining. Can you lend me something more suitable?"

Bernadette beamed, as Camilla had known she would. "Come and choose," she entreated, rising eagerly to her feet and ushering Camilla swiftly to the door. "I will tell you who is invited."

Del Amberley seemed as pleased to see Camilla as had been Bernadette; he looked forward to an interesting evening. His sister-in-law was always welcome in his house and the combination of both her and his father usually sparked off some lively discussions. He thought she looked tired tonight. For Bernadette's sake he wished she would give up this nursing, although he respected her determination to be independent.

Sir Walter Amberley was a little more restrained in his welcome; he had not known that Camilla was to dine with them and would have preferred it otherwise. It wasn't that he disliked her exactly, but he always had the sneaking feeling that she liked to get the better of him when they met. He didn't think much at all of women who were as self-sufficient as Camilla; he liked his women to be docile and dependent like Bernadette. He would be on his guard tonight, perhaps even try a few tricks himself; he would like to see Camilla brought to heel.

Camilla had not expected Sir Walter to be in town, and viewed his presence with mixed feelings. She had determined that at their first meeting she would enlighten him as to the dreadful conditions in St Giles. This evening she was quite unprepared for such a formidable task. Had she really the courage to involve such a man? She took a deep breath, concluded that courage simply must be found and steeled herself to get him alone.

The occasion, however, did not present itself easily. She began to have niggling doubts. Was this after all the right time? He had readily donated to

St Thomas's when she had first begun her training, but suggesting that the homes of St Giles were in any way his responsibility, simply because he was wealthy enough to do something about it, was hardly polite.

Emma and Melissa Buchanan, daughters of Del's Oxfordshire neighbour whose family was also in town, both gave piano recitals and sang somewhat inadequately to their captive audience. This custom was something Camilla abhorred. As her own voice lacked talent she had always refused to inflict its tones on other people. The young ladies' brother, however, proved to be far more interesting.

Alexander Buchanan was twenty-six, an ex-admirer of Bernadette and close friend of Del. Camilla had met him on only a few occasions before but she admitted to herself now, that he was, if not handsome, then tolerably goodlooking. His hair was fair, almost the colour of straw; he wore a moustache over his rather sensitive mouth. His manners, she perceived, were impeccable, his conversation witty. Her ego took an upward bound as his attention to her increased, and the evening progressed, St Giles became further and further from her mind.

Alexander Buchanan, who was, he claimed with some pride, a distant relative of the ex-president James Buchanan of America, surprised her by inviting her to be his guest in the family box at the opera. Delighted, she accepted. During dinner they became quite absorbed in a discussion on the works of the modern writer Thomas Hardy. Their conversation, however, was suddenly interrupted.

"Would you like to come, Miss Haddesley?" Sir Walter, a bald headed man whose face was framed by white Dundreary whiskers, called out.

As Camilla had not heard his remark, he repeated it, a broad grin creasing his face. "There is an exhibition of Russian Fleas being held at five, Leicester Square. I thought you might be interested." He took out a bill from his pocket and slipping in his monocle with much wrinkling of his rather large nose, he began to read: "*'Exhibiting daily from one till ten, fleas of many countries'*." He ignored the raised faces around the table. The Misses Buchanan, having thought themselves to have misheard what he said, were trying to work out any words ending in E A S, which might be appropriate. Del, knowing his father better, raised his eyebrows and waited.

"*'Firing Cannons, stage coach ride. Marconi's Flying Flea Circus. Admission one shilling'*. What about it, Miss Haddesley? I'll even escort you if you wish to go." His confidence that she would decline his offer came through in his voice.

Bernadette cringed with disgust. Del glanced around his guests with furtive embarrassment. His father knew perfectly well that this was no subject for the dinner table. The Misses Buchanan having had their worst fears confirmed had both paled to a yellowish shade of white. Their brother, having a rather stronger stomach, sat back in his chair eyeing Camilla, wondering how she would answer what might be taken as a provocative insult.

Quite unperturbed she raised her eyebrows in mock surprise. She knew full well that he was taunting her, hoping to see her colour rise, and her eyes light up with anger. Well, now he had asked for it. She had thought to spare him this move tonight. Yes, her anger was kindled; he knew perfectly well that she saw enough fleas in one day to furnish six circuses. Only the day before she had caught one with wet soap on her own bed. She dropped her eyes coyly, before lifting them, heavy lidded, to his round, expectant face.

"Well, that really is most interesting, Sir Walter. I would be absolutely fascinated to see if there is any difference between Russian and British fleas. I shall accept your invitation with delight . . . but on one condition."

The footman, who was pouring wine into Sir Walter's glass at the time, could not resist a swift glance at Camilla's face. Almost overfilling the glass, he received a severe rebuke from the hovering butler.

Camilla felt the eyes of the party upon her. Sir Walter reddened, spluttered inarticulately, but dare not withdraw his offer. Del was watching her with laughter lit eyes although his face remained as solemn as mourning. Bernadette glanced feverishly from one to the other recognizing that glint of devilment in Camilla's eye. Alexander Buchanan still watched his companion with undisguised admiration. He found her more and more interesting as the minutes went by.

Camilla touched her mouth lightly with her serviette then laid it slowly on the table. Sir Walter leaned back on his chair, smoothed his moustache, then coughed.

"If you are to show me Russian fleas, then I must insist that you allow me to show you some magnificent British ones, Sir Walter!"

"Bravo!" Del could contain his humour no longer. "Why that's uncommonly decent of you, Camilla! I am sure, Sir, that you are absolutely dying to compare their size. Is that not so, Sir?"

Camilla could have kissed him right there and then. The Buchanan sisters were still looking thoroughly disgusted by the whole conversation and really Camilla did not blame them.

Sir Walter looked shrewdly, first out of one eye then out of the other. His monocle dropped on its chain unobserved. The joke had bounced back on him, and he knew it. But how should he take it? Should he bluster the whole thing off as hilarious, good-humoured banter? He was most unsure. That Camilla was serious he had no doubt and he suspected he had fallen right bang into her trap.

She saw his suspicious look. He was wondering what she was after this time.

His opinion that there were too many men already squandering public funds was no secret, nor was his criticism that Mr Rathbone was always wanting more and more spent on the poor. As far as Sir Walter was concerned the poor should damn well look after themselves. She was acutely aware of the difficulty of the task she had set herself.

Scowling now, he took a comforting sip of the wine. Good wine this, first rate. His son always kept a good cellar. He smiled slightly to himself; look who taught him! The movement of a white, linen napkin just a little to his left brought his mind swiftly back to the problem in hand. He smiled again, this time at Camilla.

"Well, my dear, and where do you keep these British fleas?" His eyes twinkled suddenly. "You don't have them with you, I presume?"

Alexander nearly choked on the wine he was drinking; then he let out a loud roar of laughter. Camilla took it well, she knew that now she had to play her cards very carefully. A good joke, a good laugh to divulge in the genial atmosphere of their club was all it was to the men. To the girls, an unpleasant discussion to be shuddered over and forgotten as soon as possible. To the people of St Giles; her people, her patients and growingly her friends, it could mean hope.

She sighed slowly, murmuring a quiet "Thank you!" to the maid for the strawberries and cream that were placed in front of her. In the background the butler moved about sternly, looking quite unconcerned at the topic over dinner, but giving the occasional cough as one of the maids took too much interest.

"Well!" Camilla sighed. "I suppose it would be really too much to expect of you, Sir Walter. A man of your customs and stamina might not be up to it!"

"Up to what, up to what?" he almost shouted. That had done it; she had questioned his manhood; he was wide awake now, eager for battle with a spoon in his hand and a lace serviette at his throat.

Camilla, disinclined to be hurried, tasted the cream and nodded approvingly towards Bernadette. "Beautiful, darling!" she murmured. "But then," she continued, directing her remarks to Sir Walter again, and sensing the tension rising in the room — "the Duke of Westminster; he's our chairman you know — " she imparted graciously to the Misses Emma and Melissa Buchanan, who nodded in unison — "the Duke of Westminster — " she repeated — "and the Earl of Dalhousie, Lord Lyttleton, Mr Henry Bonham Carter, Mr Guy . . . " She did not finish, Sir Walter rose from his chair took two rapid steps towards the door then retreated and sat down again very abruptly.

"All right, all right, Miss Haddesley, and what would you have me do that these noteworthy gentlemen have inevitably done before?"

Whether the members of the Association Committee had actually walked the courts of St Giles she had no idea, but then she had not actually said they had. She smiled sweetly; a promise given in anger might not hold. Sir Walter was a gentleman but he would not be made a fool of by a woman.

"Oh, really, Sir Walter, I cannot hold you to such a tenuous joke, but I would be most divinely grateful if you would take a look at some houses with me?"

"Look at some houses! Buying property are you?" he exclaimed, absent-mindedly putting in his monocle to peer across the table at her.

"Not exactly, but I would greatly value your opinion," she put in rapidly, gleaning every advantage like an experienced politician.

He was still waiting for the card, the trump card he most dreaded, yet without his knowledge it had already been played. He looked suspicious now, wondering. "And where are these houses that are of so much interest to you?" he demanded.

"Quite near to Bloomsbury Square. Why we could walk the distance easily," she told him lightly.

He laughed, smoothed his whiskers with both hands and then began to attack his strawberries and cream.

The tension fell away like a cast-off gown, Camilla continued with her own meal knowing full well that in this round at least, she had won.

Alexander Buchanan leaned a little closer to her and whispered softly in her ear.

"How close?" he asked meaningfully.

She turned to look at him, eyebrows raised. "I beg your pardon," she asked demurely.

"These houses," he inquired, still keeping his voice low." How near to Bloomsbury Square are they?"

She shrugged. "Oh, just a little way. Over Oxford Street and . . . " She felt as if she were dancing on a precipice.

"St Giles?" he suggested knowingly,

his eyes sparkling with humour.

She nodded, dreading he was going to give her away.

The grin that curved his lips and lit his dark eyes made him most attractive, she thought suddenly, forgetting for a moment her delicately balanced position and feeling a little lightheaded by her eloquent success. "You are going to make him inspect the slums of St Giles," he persisted, watching her out of the corner of his eye. "Why, by jove! I should like to be there!"

"Then come, too," she suggested briskly. She doubted in her own mind if he even went below stairs into the servants' quarters of his own home. And they would be a palace compared with St Giles!

4

A DARK gunmetal cloud burst suddenly over St Giles. Camilla was unsure at first whether to bless it or curse it. What glorious sunshine they had enjoyed in the days before! She looked down now at the water which ran in wide channels from the courts and ended in large boggy areas of floating debris at the entrance to each one.

Rain made the whole district more difficult to cross, every step was a carefully planned manoeuvre. On the other hand, rain freshened the air, and for once Camilla would have preferred that St Giles stank as it did on the hottest summer day. On this day, she was a little afraid of Sir Walter.

She was glad Alexander Buchanan was coming. Sir Walter would hardly opt out of his promise with him present.

Alexander had arrived full of good-humour as if he intended to enjoy the visit, though Camilla thought that most unlikely. His well-cut, broadcloth coat was of a dark blue; his waistcoat white, embroidered elaborately with gold silk. He did indeed cut a fine figure, so startlingly out of place in those meagre surroundings, even to his cane, silver topped in the shape of an acorn. What an attractive man he was!

Sir Walter, equally smart, but more subdued in his attire was wearing a suit of dark brown. The only glimmer of lightness in his dress was his white cravat and the shimmering silver of his whiskers. He, too, carried a cane, a stouter one than Alexander, and Camilla could not determine its design for its tip was grasped very firmly in his rather plump hand. From the moment he had arrived he had that 'let's get it over with' look in his eye. His face had registered only displeasure when their walk had crossed Oxford Street and proceeded in the direction of St

Giles. He was already wondering why the devil he had agreed to this fiasco.

Camilla had already pointed out the closeness of the houses; the obliteration of light that resulted. Sir Walter grunted, fingered his whiskers but made no comment. When she stepped through the brick built archway Camilla had it all planned. She would play the two against each other, defying one to decline to enter a house when the other might do so. Sadly, she was aware that she could be losing an admirer. Alexander knew so little of her work although they had discussed it briefly over dinner, but how much of what it entailed had he really understood?

She found herself thinking how much easier it would be to walk this way with Dr Grantly by her side. How much less terrifying the thought that the rotten stairs might give way under his weight than that of the stocky Sir Walter. He was remaining silent, but Camilla was beginning to wish that he would shout at her. This stony silence was unbearable. Scowling now, he kicked out a boot at a scraggy mongrel that had been yapping at his feet. The dog yelped in pain and scuttled, tail down, into one of the houses.

Alexander smiled wanly at Camilla. "By jove," he said, as if something must be said, but the appropriate sentiment escaped him. Surely she wasn't expecting them to actually go inside these shacks. Why there was no knowing what one might pick up; fleas at the very least.

Heart pounding, Camilla walked on.

Sir Walter turned around, and stalked out through the arch again.

Alexander, quite unable to follow Camilla himself because the stench was so vile, called her name, getting out his own kerchief to cover his nose. When she appeared in the doorway he waved his arm in the direction of the street, before leaving himself.

Camilla, filled with sudden anger raced after him, lifting her skirts and calling loudly Sir Walter's name.

"Have you no feelings at all?" she shouted angrily. "Do you not care that these people live in such places when a man like you could change it all?"

Sir Walter stormed on down the street, neither hearing nor caring what she said. That was the last time he took any notice of a woman! When Camilla burst out on to the street she saw only his plump figure in the distance, hurrying away from her. For a moment she stood seething with rage; her face quite red, her pulse racing. Then, suddenly, she saw Alexander.

He was standing on the cobbled road, staring around him at the clutter of chimney pots and the score upon score of crowded dwellings. She approached him slowly, her anger subsiding at the sight of his paleness. Surely it had been unforgivable of her to subject him to such humiliation without adequate warning. She expected nothing but rebuke; perhaps it was all she deserved. The hopes she had, the plans she had dreamed of, were shattered in pieces on that cobbled street. She was bitterly, bitterly disappointed.

Alexander smiled. It was not the warm, charming smile to which she had become accustomed, but a faint, apologetic smile, rather wan and doing nothing for the pasty colour of his cheeks.

A short distance away a black cloaked figure leaned wearily against the wall, listening.

"I have disappointed you," Alexander said. "My apologies!"

She did not answer straight away; his words surprised her.

He waved an arm vaguely around him. "You had hoped to persuade Sir Walter that he should do something about these . . . these hovels."

She nodded slowly; he had understood. "I believe Sir Walter could rebuild them if he wished."

He frowned. "But surely Sir Walter does not own them?"

"Would it trouble him much to purchase the street? He would spend as much in refurnishing one of his houses!" She wished at once that she had not added those words; it seemed a little disloyal to Bernadette. Alexander was bound to know about Mr Morris's changes to her house.

"You consider he should share a little of his great wealth with those who have nothing?"

"Exactly!" she said vehemently. "To these people it would mean a new life. We can show them how to keep their homes cleaner, how to care for their children better, but how can they be happy, contented families when they live in such boxes with no clean air to freshen the clothes they do wash?"

For a moment he stood looking down into her eyes, then he shook his head very slowly. "I admired you last week at Cleveland Row, Miss Haddesley. After what I have seen today I can but admire you twice as much. My own fortunes are, alas, tied up until I marry. My father," he laughed lightly, "he would be of the same mind as Sir Walter."

"Mr Buchanan," she put in hurriedly. "It was at your own request that you came, but I am most concerned that it made you ill. I trust you are feeling better now."

"Very much better, thank you," he replied quietly then he turned swiftly as a shout rang out over the street.

Camilla swung around, too, knowing the voice at once. Robbie Gower ran full tilt along the road, ignoring the swelling water, getting soaked to his knees as he stepped uncaring into deep, muddy puddles. "Nurse!" he shouted again. "Nurse! The doctor wants you. He says to tell you to come quick, please!"

She looked up apologetically at Alexander. Was that relief she saw in his eyes?

"I must go," she said, quickly moving away. Then she called back to him: "Thank you, thank you for coming."

He lifted a hand in acknowledgement, donning his silk hat and gloves.

"Remember," he shouted, "the opera!"

She smiled, a little surprised. "Goodbye, Mr Buchanan."

He watched her go, a lady in a trim, blue cloak and bonnet stepping swiftly around the flooded ruts, a lady who, despite his gallant words, he was beginning to wish had chosen to spend her time elsewhere.

Camilla self-consciously straightened her bonnet as she entered the court to which Robbie had directed her. It was not unusual for him to take messages for Dr Grantly; indeed it was becoming the custom. Since a brief talk she had had with the doctor about young Robbie's hopes of saving up to buy a barrow and becoming a coster, almost all the messages from St Giles were brought by Robbie Gower. He had also returned to his newspaper stand.

A large rat shot out of the doorway as she moved inside, and was followed swiftly by a scraggy, grey cat. For a brief moment she stopped to compose her thoughts and put out of her mind the sense of failure that overwhelmed her. Then, hurriedly, she went inside where she found Dr Grantly struggling to suture a deep cut in a woman's leg.

"Gad, I'm glad to see you, Nurse Haddesley!" he exclaimed, his face quite red with exasperation, and ducking to miss a clenched fist. "I fear I cannot manage without help. The neighbours say she has the pox and they will not come in." Again the woman kicked, knocking his arm and spilling a bowl of disinfectant. "Gad, madam! — " he shouted angrily — "lie still, I beg you."

Camilla moved beside him and began talking to the woman and calming her. How thin were her hands; her arms! How aged her face, etched so deeply with lines of care and pain. Yet it was doubtful she was more than forty years. Now she was still, hearing a woman's voice, feeling the comfort as Camilla took a little water and washed her fevered brow. Dr Grantly proceeded to insert the sutures with a great deal more success.

"Is the woman's family not here?" she asked.

He glanced swiftly down at Camilla's face, then he sighed deeply and smiled. "I have sent for her husband."

"Does she have the pox?" Camilla enquired doubtfully.

"I believe not, the rash is too fine. I think it a case of some food poisoning mingled with the terror from her injury." His eyes moved to the woman's face and he shook his head slowly. "See how at ease she is now that you have come. She knows from your voice that you are a woman; from your uniform that you are her friend. I think sometimes that it might be advantageous if doctors wore some kind of garb that would mark them, at least as not an enemy." He laughed, the strain quite gone from his face now. "Perhaps you would care to design some kind of uniform for me?"

92

"A distinguished one, of course," she said, longing to look up at his face but not daring even to lift her eyes. The room was so small and they were standing so close together that when he moved he touched her arm. How tall he is, she thought, yes, taller than Alexander. And how handsome are those dark brown eyes, yet I dare not look into them although I know they are full of laughter now.

"Why of course," he said loftily. "The cut of a gentleman; a necessity I feel."

"Then I have it," she announced quite straightfaced. "A tall silk hat, trousers of small grey and white check, a black, 'University' coat, I believe it is called, a slim black necktie and . . . ah, a plum waistcoat to add a touch of colour." She glanced quickly at his face now, wondering suddenly if he might be offended.

She had described with complete accuracy the attire he was wearing, but although his eyes were on the bandage, they were still crinkled with laughter.

"You are a genius, Miss Haddesley!" he exclaimed, as she leaned over to place the covers over the woman's leg. She slept soundly now, quite unaware of the frivolous conversation at her bedside; exhausted by her struggling and pain. "Sheer genius!" he continued. "But then I have always known it to be so. Anyone with hair so radiant in colour must surely be the most brilliant of women."

From the shadows of the doorway a figure clad in a black cloak crept away unnoticed. The brow, well hidden by the hood was furrowed, the lips tight with anger. As Mrs Germain cast a last upward glance at the window above her a peal of frivolous laughter floated out making her scowl all the more. Her recent attempts to discredit Miss Haddesley seemed to have failed. Stronger measures were obviously needed.

Camilla had great difficulty in

concealing her laughter. It was really too bad of him to flaunt his humour beside the bed of this poor, sick woman, yet even at that moment she knew how much they both needed humour to survive those tragic houses.

When the woman's husband arrived, Dr Grantly was still there. He should by rights have left but he seemed reluctant to do so, taking the woman's pulse on several occasions and pacing the room with an air of impatience. As Camilla explained to the husband about his wife's condition and treatment, Dr Grantly suddenly took his leave of them, rather to Camilla's disappointment. She was not totally surprised, however, when stepping out into the street, she found him waiting.

"I've sent young Robbie for a cab," he told her as if his presence needed some explanation. Then, as if in afterthought, he said: "Oh, do you not have a lecture this afternoon?"

She confirmed that she had, pulling her cloak tightly around herself as if to prepare to walk away.

"Then may I escort you home? I assume you are due back at Bloomsbury Square very shortly."

Her expectation of this invitation did nothing to hide her embarrassment, "Why, yes," she stuttered almost inaudibly. "But I really can walk!" If he had agreed that she do so, she would never have forgiven herself. The half humorous thought she had had all those weeks ago about setting her cap at James Grantly and playing a game of competition with his housekeeper was very far from her mind. The desire she had now to get to know him better was no ploy to find a husband but a genuine liking for his company. Alexander Buchanan faded discreetly into the background in her currently fickle mind.

"I will not hear of it," he declared, much to her relief. "Ah, here it is at last!"

When they were comfortably settled in the cab, he turned towards her with his own peculiar lop-sided grin. "I'm sure the cab man will allow you to alight on the opposite side of the square if you prefer it?"

"If you please," she answered, glad of his discretion.

He called up to the cabby, then sighed deeply. "Well now, Miss Haddesley, and how is life treating you at the Association?"

She replied that she was enjoying it greatly and oddly enough found she really meant it. Her fears of being attacked after the incident with Alfred Hackett had greatly diminished. Before they reached the square, however, she found herself pouring out the whole story of Del's father and her hope for St Giles.

"A great disappointment for you," he said gently, his face lit with sympathy. "I can indeed understand how you must feel, my dear Miss Haddesley." For a moment his eyes, almost hidden by the shadows of the cab, held hers, then, as if some sudden decision had been made, he smiled and tilted his head to one side. "In fact, I do believe a little cheering up is called for. I wonder, would you do me the honour of dining with me this evening?" It was a rash request he knew, if it were to be made known, the gossiping tongues would begin for sure, but suddenly he did not care.

The cab had halted; the horse stamped its hoof impatiently on the road but he did not seem to notice.

"I'd be delighted," she answered in a whisper, wanting to pinch herself to see she was not dreaming.

"Seven o'clock, er . . . perhaps on Bloomsbury Way?"

She smiled and nodded. "Thank you, and thank you for the ride," she added, remembering with embarrassment that first cab ride together.

"My pleasure, Miss Haddesley, I assure you," he said, unfastening the apron to allow her to descend. Then he leaned a little out of the cab and said quietly. "I am relieved you do not think me such an ogre now."

She turned, startled, and looking up into his face, saw the twinkle in his eye, then she blushed, and thanking the cabby with great haste she hurried away not even looking up when the horse trotted past her, yet knowing quite well that he would watch her through the window as he went.

If she had wished for something pleasant to end a day of heart-breaking disappointment she could not have wished for anything other than to dine with James Grantly. Her only regret was that she must keep it a secret. How she would have loved to boast the fact to the other girls over luncheon.

By that afternoon her anger with Sir Walter had vanished completely, although she still felt disillusioned at her own failure. The lecture had been interesting; the prospect of dinner that evening was positively exciting. Now she was walking across Hyde Park in the warm sunshine, and as she had some fifteen minutes to wait before her appointment she spent it watching the horses canter along Rotten Row.

It reminded her rather acutely that if she were to marry Alexander then her life would become once more a life of leisure, of riding most certainly; something she readily admitted she missed. She sighed and turned away from the hoof-marked sand. What indecision she found in her own mind, how fickle her emotions as they swayed to and fro between the two men. Two men so different, not only in their appearance but also in their outlook on life. She tried to pretend she had a real choice, that both had proposed marriage to her and she could choose at will. But the truth invaded her dreams; reality won, neither had made any such proposal and if the past were anything to go by then nor would they.

She was suddenly aware of the sound of traffic in the distance and looking at her timepiece found she must hurry on to reach her destination in time. It was not the first occasion she had been invited to South Street to have tea with Miss Florence Nightingale and there was nothing unusual about that at all. Miss Nightingale kept in touch with all of the nurses at her training school and when they left she preferred to have a hand in their choice of position. Camilla had received a long letter of encouragement when she had first gone to Bloomsbury Square and had corresponded with her ever since.

Firmly she lifted the knocker of number ten South Street and tapped it down lightly on the door. A man-servant answered the door and she stepped inside to be shown into a white walled, drawing room where a lady sat writing at her desk. She was attired in a black silk dress with fine, white Buckinghamshire lace.

Miss Nightingale did not look up immediately but continued to work for a moment, then she took an envelope, folded the paper carefully, slipped it inside and sealed it before placing it in an already overflowing tray on her desk. Then, when she had brushed the plump, black cat off her lap she crossed to sit in an arm chair inviting Camilla to do likewise. The cat miaowed disappointedly and crept away towards the small fire. There it scrapped playfully with the large tabby who had until that minute been sleeping peacefully on the hearthrug.

How strange it was, Camilla thought, enjoying the scent of fresh flowers in the room, that since her return from the Crimea twenty-two years ago, Miss Nightingale had made neither public statement or appearance. She had returned home a heroine, had songs written about her, been summoned to audiences with Queen Victoria, yet few of the soldiers she had nursed, or their families, even knew she was still alive today. A man Camilla had nursed herself had been in Miss Nightingale's care all those years before at the Scutari Hospital.

"Never heard what happened to her," he had said. "Did she pass on?"

When Camilla had told him that she was very much alive, despite severe collapse and exhaustion, and years of illness, he had insisted on dictating a letter to thank her for her work.

Not that Miss Nightingale had stopped working. The actual practical nursing side had finished, but since her return in eighteen fifty-six she had laboured unceasingly against all physical odds in compiling of statistics, drawing up of regulations, working for the reform of military hospitals.

"We use her expert advice daily," an acquaintance of Camilla's at the War Department had told her. "She advises not only secretaries but also Ministers of State."

"You have a brother in India," Miss Nightingale said when the first welcome and general remarks had been made.

"Why, yes, indeed," Camilla replied, surprised that she should have remembered, although Miss Nightingale's concern for India was well known.

A bundle of fur sprang suddenly on

to her knee. She disliked cats but it seemed impolite to push it away so she rubbed the back of its ear gently and it lay there purring softly.

Miss Nightingale sighed. "Oh, that I could do something more for India! My dear Lord Salisbury left the India office in April, and to be brutally truthful, Camilla my influence there has not been the same since. There are times when it seems quite, quite impossible to obtain the details I need. I have asked for the figures relating to the famine, but they will not allow me the records." She shook her head and sighed again. "But I shall persist, my dear Camilla. They will not put me off."

Camilla brushed the hairs off her knee as the fat tabby slipped down on to the carpet to drink at the large dish of milk. "You will win though in the end, Miss Nightingale," she assured her hostess firmly. "Although I'm sure it must be most frustrating for you to have so much opposition to everything you do. But look at what you have achieved; the conditions in British Hospitals alone have improved tremendously through your persistence."

"Years of persistence, my dear; years of sheer, hard work. And yet, I feel I have achieved nothing. To be truthful, when I returned from the Crimea, quite determined to do something for the Military Hospitals, I imagined civil hospitals were better, but, oh, what delusion! They were, if anything, worse." She sighed, then a soft smile lit her face. "But then I see you; and if only you knew what sheer joy it is to see the perpetuation of my ideas for nursing in such beautiful young ladies as your dear self, then you would see that I do have something for which I must thank God."

A maid knocked then came in with the tea.

Miss Nightingale thanked her graciously, lifting a small, silver jug. "Now, do you take cream with your tea?"

Camilla said she did. How odd it

was that there was no feeling of awe when one visited Miss Nightingale. Such a truly great lady, one whom she herself so admired and revered, yet one conversed with her as one might a fellow probationer.

It was Miss Nightingale who spoke next. "There are little lines on your face, my dear. Tell me, how are you finding district nursing? Miss Lees tells me your work is highly satisfactory; she recommends that you continue with her after training. Does that comply with your own feelings on the matter?"

"It is what I hoped for, Miss Nightingale!" she replied.

"Dr James Grantly!" Miss Nightingale said slowly.

Camilla knew to her horror that her cheeks were suddenly burning like fire.

Miss Nightingale smiled, more to herself than to Camilla. "A most efficient physician; I remember him well when he was at St Thomas's. I found him exceedingly courteous and most agreeable. Let me see he must be all of thirty by now. My, how time flies!" Then she leaned forward and patted Camilla's hand. "He, too, speaks very highly of your work, I understand."

Camilla said nothing, she was quite astounded that James Grantly made reports to Miss Lees, yet it was, of course, a sensible arrangement.

"And how do you yourself view the good doctor, my dear?" her hostess inquired with a look in her eye that said quite clearly that she really needed no answer. Camilla knew only too well that Miss Nightingale was known for her continual interest in her nurses; they all talked to her quite openly about their doubts, their fears and also, it appeared, their loves.

Suddenly Camilla found she was no exception. All at once she was pouring out the whole story of her concern for St Giles and her attempt to get Sir Walter to make changes. And even more surprisingly, the way her heart fluttered whenever she was near Dr Grantly. That she should admit the fact to Miss Nightingale was quite astonishing; even more so considering she had scarcely admitted it to herself.

When the interview was over, she was left with a feeling of complete satisfaction. Her failure with Sir Walter was just a little setback; there would be other opportunities. "These little trials are sent to strengthen our determination, dear," she had been told. "District Nurses are like sanitary missionaries, and whilst they must be concerned and prayerful about their patients, they are not almsgivers; their knowledge and experience are far more valuable than any loaf of bread."

"I have great confidence in you, my dear Camilla," she had said as her guest was handed the traditional cake before leaving. Then a twinkle had come into her eye as she laid a gentle hand on Camilla's arm. "And don't be misled by other wealthy gentlemen who may wish to marry you!" She smiled almost to herself. "Yes, Dr Grantly seemed an agreeably pleasant young man."

There was a lightness in Camilla's step as she walked down South Streeet towards Park Lane. She was free until her engagement with Dr Grantly at seven o'clock; she decided to take the opportunity to visit Bernadette.

The breeze had dropped as she turned into Piccadilly, and found her way across Green Park. She was looking forward to talking with her sister but found herself hoping that Alexander would not be there.

Bernadette, however was full of Mr William Morris who had dined with them again on the previous evening. Oh, how she rambled on about the pre-Raphaelite brotherhood. Camilla felt quite angry that her own eventful day was of so little importance to her sister. Desperately she tried to muster up interest in the writings and arts of those gentlemen, but her own pre-occupation with St Giles, Miss Nightingale and dear Dr Grantly loomed far greater in her mind.

Eventually she lost all patience with Bernadette and snapped quite loudly that she had heard enough of Mr Morris. At once she knew she had been unkind; Bernadette was quite hurt and Camilla regretted her outburst immediately and apologised. The visit to Miss Nightingale failed to impress, however. Rossetti's poetry, the new bathing costume of scarlet flannel edged with torchon lace which Bernadette had purchased for a coming visit to Hastings, and the recently installed gas geyser were far more important in the life of Mrs Delano Amberley. Camilla felt most disappointed.

Del was dining at The Carlton Club in Pall Mall with Alexander that evening but both men arrived at the house shortly after Camilla. They had been shooting on a friend's estate just outside London and were both attired accordingly. Camilla was rather amused by Del's coat, a loosely fitting, woollen jacket, short in length and edged with grey fur. Its colour, dark green, was reflected in the green and light grey check of his trousers. The hat he carried was of black felt with a small, round brim. Alexander's brown and fawn checked suit seemed positively plain beside it, although his small-brimmed, brown bowler which curved up at the sides was the height of fashion for such occasions.

Camilla dutifully confirmed that she would be delighted to accompany Alexander to the Savoy Theatre on the following Friday evening. She would have preferred to back out of the invitation really, but did not want to appear rude.

"Do come and see our geyser," Del was saying. "And you, too, Camilla. And I have ordered one of those gramophone contraptions."

How Camilla laughed, Del was always wanting to try out new inventions. His house had been the first in St

James to install gas lighting. And now it seemed they had a geyser, a Rapid Water Heater, and he was determined that his guests should share his excitement.

Camilla followed her sister down the basement stairs into the kitchens below. The geyser was fixed by a bracket on to a scrubbed, wooden table by the window. It was already lit, but Del put out a hand to extinguish the pilot light.

"You will need one of these one day, Camilla," he called across to her. "It's time you were thinking of getting married, you know. You can't do this nursing thing for the rest of your life!"

Camilla ignored his remark, knowing Del well enough to take it in good humour, but she still felt annoyed at the comment in front of Alexander. She felt his eyes on her but she turned her head away quickly.

Del turned on the gas tap and struck a match which did not light.

Another match glowed in his fingers. He spoke to Alexander with a laugh. "Father was livid about St Giles, you know. Say's he'll never trust a woman again." He glanced at Camilla and smiled. "Don't you believe a word of it, Camilla, he'll come around, you see!" He moved his arm towards the water heater, touching the burner with a tiny light. At once, there was an enormous bang. Bernadette screamed. Flames leapt from the burner catching Del on his fur edged cuff. In terror he began to run, shaking his arm as the flames darted towards his shoulder. Alexander, with great presence of mind, reached out and turned off the tap to exclude more gas, and prevent the curtains from catching alight.

Camilla ran forward, meeting Del as he reached the doorway and made as if to run through. Deftly, she grabbed him by the jacket, attempting to throw him on to the floor. But he began to struggle, wrenching himself away from her as if he could run away from the flames. They were licking his hair by now and the fur on his coat smelled terrible as it burned. His face was contorted by pain and horror. She knew she had to stop him, had to get him down to the floor. Bernadette was shouting his name, screaming instructions that he neither heard nor heeded. Then she fainted across the doorway, striking her head on the door jamb. Swiftly Camilla put out her foot, Del tripped and with tremendous effort she had him down and was rolling him in the kitchen rug.

Alexander stared, hopelessly unsure what to do next. As the flames began to die out, Camilla shouted: "Send for Dr Grantly, twenty-three, Russell Square. And get some servants to help me!"

Without answering he was gone. The butler appeared almost immediately with several maids and the houseboy not far behind. Bernadette, who was still unconscious, lay motionless on the stone slab floor. Camilla's instructions were followed without comment.

Bernadette was carried to her own room. Del, now calmer, but suffering inevitably from shock, lay still, his breathing fast, his skin sweating and pale. She grabbed several tablecloths from the drawer in the kitchen table and wrapped them around him. Then he, too, was carried upstairs.

It seemed to Camilla only minutes before the sound of horses' hooves clattered rapidly on the road; the carriage had returned bringing James Grantly. She was greatly relieved.

"Why, Miss Haddesly!" he exclaimed on seeing her by Del's bed.

She looked up and smiled wanly. "I have presumed greatly on your kindness. I know this area is not usually in your care, but Bernadette is my sister. You were simply the first physician that came to my mind."

He smiled, then looked down at Del. "I am glad your opinion of my work is so favourable," he said.

He did not speak again until he had thoroughly examined both Del

115

and Bernadette "Your sister, as I'm sure you have concluded, is suffering from mild concussion," he told her.

She nodded. "I have recorded her pulse rate on the paper by the bed. It is very slow but had improved to sixty beats per minute on the last occasion."

As he looked at her, such a strange look came into his eyes; was it pain?

Camilla glanced away, her own thoughts quite disarranged for a moment. What did it mean, that expression of anguish? What thoughts had prompted the appearance of those furrowed lines on his brow?

"There is little to be done," he said, bringing her thoughts back to the sickroom. "Just watch and wait. She is not in deep coma; I am of the opinion that she will regain consciousness quite soon."

His words proved correct, Bernadette recovered rapidly and a nurse was sent for to remain with Del.

When everything was settled, Camilla

glanced at her watch. A quarter from seven.

"I have a notion that our dinner engagement would perhaps be better postponed," a quiet voice said beside her. "I doubt you are in the mood for dinner conversation even with me."

She thanked him and suggested he go down for coffee in the library. As Cook had refused to go into the kitchen until the geyser was removed she could not offer him dinner there at Cleveland Row. A workman had been sent for to disconnect the gas and take the wretched thing away.

In the library Dr Grantly discovered a very perturbed Alexander, whom everyone had forgotten, pacing the floor and greatly annoyed that no one had bothered to keep him informed. Within half an hour a Nurse Rawlings, a contemporary of Camilla's whom she knew to be reliable, was installed. Camilla joined the gentlemen downstairs.

"Why, you look quite worn out, Camilla, my dear!" Alexander exclaimed, using her Christian name for the first time.

She laughed lightly. "Oh, I shall be well enough after a good night's sleep. I confess I do feel a little tired, although really I do not deserve to be today."

"Why, what nonsense you do talk!" Alexander exclaimed. Then looking at James Grantly, he went on. "Are you aware, me dear sir, that this young lady works her fingers to the bone, nursing sick people in St Giles?" He shook his head and sighed. "And in what conditions she works, in what fearful conditions!"

Camilla glanced discreetly at James Grantly and saw a smile on his face. She would leave it to him to answer that one.

"Ah, indeed, I am aware of it, Mr Buchanan," he said with slow deliberation. "Why, we were working together only this morning were we not, Miss Haddesley?"

Camilla nodded. She could see that Alexander was annoyed, but he made some effort to hide it. He disliked being scored off like that especially by a mere physician. He got to his feet, strolled around the room for a few moments, scrutinized a few books on the shelves then sat down again suddenly.

"You trained as a physician in London Dr Grantly?" he asked, removing the subject of St Giles from the conversation.

Camilla saw dislike in his eyes for James Grantly, she did not relish any disagreement between these two.

"Yes, indeed, like Miss Haddesley I trained at St Thomas's."

Again the connection between them. Alexander's moustache drooped slightly at the corners. He was still wearing his check suit from the afternoon's outing and was acutely aware that he was wrongly dressed for the time of day.

"I worked for a period afterwards under Professor Lister at King's College," Dr Grantly went on. "He was appointed Professor of Clinical Surgery there last year. In fact, may I suggest

Miss Haddesley, that tomorrow we call in Professor Lister to look at your brother-in-law's arm? If necessary he may wish to transfer him to his nursing home at Fifteen, Fitzroy Square."

"Why, yes, of course!" agreed Camilla eagerly. "Do ask Professor Lister to come and I will prepare the servants to receive him."

"Gladly, ma'am," he replied. "And in fact I shall be attending one of Professor Lister's lectures at King's College on Friday evening."

She sat up eagerly. "Why, how interesting! I have always wished to hear him speak. You must tell me all about it afterwards."

He smiled warmly and laid his clasped hands on the table. "If you really are interested, then may I suggest you accompany me? The ladies will no doubt be in the minority but there will be others there."

Alexander coughed. "I'm afraid Miss Haddesley is already engaged on Friday evening," he put in hurriedly. "We are going to the Savoy are we not, Camilla? I have the tickets here in my notecase." His hand fumbled in his pocket but he did not produce them.

Camilla, her mouth open to answer Dr Grantly with pure delight, closed it abruptly. She was furious, absolutely furious. She doubted very much that Alexander had the tickets at all. He had only asked her that evening and could undoubtedly purchase them anytime. But alas, she could not deny that she had agreed to it, and he obviously had no intention of conceeding her company to another man, lecture on surgery or no. She checked an angry retort with difficulty.

Dr Grantly raised his eyebrows but gave no sign of the humour he felt. "Another time," he said, then glancing at his pocket watch he frowned. "I must ask you to excuse me. I have a great deal of paperwork to complete tonight. If I may escort you, Miss Haddesley I shall be honoured."

Alexander was on his feet like a rocket; ringing for the butler. "That won't be necessary, sir. I shall, of course, see Miss Haddesley home myself." There was an authority in his voice which Camilla deeply resented. Had Thompson the butler not come in at that moment, she would most certainly have protested. Who did he think he was, ringing for the butler and assuming such responsibility?

"Dr Grantly is leaving," she informed Thompson, turning her face away to hide her annoyance. "Would you please call a cab?"

The butler withdrew and she took her leave of them to take a look at Del and Bernadette. They were both sleeping peacefully; she descended with more ease of mind. Dr Grantly was then shown upstairs to pay a last call on his patients and he, too, was well satisfied with their condition and care. The cab was ready at the door; she waited rather nervously in the hall to bid him goodnight, dismissing the butler and holding his coat and hat herself.

He came downstairs slowly, paying no heed to the stairs but watching her face as she looked up towards him. He took his coat from her, then his hat and gloves.

"Thank you," she said, "thank you for coming!"

He touched her cheek gently with his finger.

"My pleasure, Miss Haddesley," he said softly. "My pleasure indeed, and I hope that one day I might have the great honour of using your first name, too, a very beautiful name, may I say."

She blushed and had to drop her eyes.

He smiled. "And I shall look forward with great delight to recounting at length, every detail of Professor Lister's lecture. I am most disappointed that you are unable to accompany me."

She lifted her eyes to his and smiled. "And I, too, sir," she said simply. "Greatly disappointed, but it was quite true that I had this . . . prior engagement." He nodded laughingly and began to put on his coat; she was glad to find him amused by Alexander's behaviour. He might have been offended.

"I understand," he said, almost in a whisper, "I had best take my leave of Mr Buchanan before he comes to seek you out. Pray do not be long out of your bed, my dear Camilla. I do not wish to find you out of sorts tomorrow."

She merely nodded and smiled, quite unable to answer him. She suspected that her name had slipped out quite unintentionally; she only hoped he would continue to use it when they were alone. And to gain that rare privacy, she would have to contrive a little, she mused.

Then, after a brief farewell to Alexander, he was striding down the steps, climbing swiftly into the waiting hansom.

Camilla stood by the window listening; listening to the fading sound of the horse's hooves on the stones. Then she sent for her own coat and allowed herself to be driven back to Bloomsbury by Alexander.

"Goodnight, Mr Buchanan," she called, hurrying up the steps.

On the following evening a bouquet arrived. She read the card with disinterest.

'*I am wretched at having incurred your displeasure. Forgive me, my dearest Miss Haddesley, I remain your most obedient servant, 'Alexander Buchanan.'*

5

"**W**ELL, I 'ope 'e's got 'is eyeful!" Mary Ware exclaimed, as she walked through Hyde Park.

"That fella over there, just look at 'im starin' at me as if I was somethin' the cat brought in!"

Alf Hackett was about to laugh, about to tell her that she was far from being that, when he caught sight of the man she was describing. Swiftly, he released her arm, then he moved a step away from her. It was an action that betrayed him more than the close proximity they had before and he knew it. He glanced at Mary and took in the bright pink dress with its deep flounces and sloping bustle. Rounded and soft that was how he would have described her. And since he had met her in the Dog and Gun on that cold, wet night when he had found Robbie Gower he had spent many hours in her company.

Dr James Grantly touched his hat as he inevitably came closer in walking along the gravel path. "Pleasant evening, Alfred!" he murmured, trying hard to keep his eyes from the shapely woman by Alfred's side.

Alf nodded automatically, his face quite pale. He glanced swiftly at Mary again, searching for words. "This is Mary," he said hurriedly, "friend of ours, like, me and the wife!"

The doctor smiled politely, doffed his hat to Mary before passing onwards down the path.

Mary's laugh must have reached him; Alf cringed with annoyance at her lack of concern.

"Friend of you and the wife, am I then? Not bleeding likely! Tell, 'er about me, do you?"

Alf clenched his fists until his knuckles were white. "Shut up, Mary, don't you know when to keep your mouth shut?"

She pouted her lips sulkily. "Oh,

lovely that is! Who's this fella then, what's so important? Don't want 'im seein' me an' you together, do yer? Not yer boss, is 'e?"

Alf shook his head then felt quite sick. Of all the people to meet, it would have to be him. He wouldn't tell Jenny, it wasn't that, he wasn't that sort. It was what the doctor thought of him that mattered; suddenly it mattered more than anything else.

Mary hitched up her skirts and sniffed. "Well, I know when I'm not wanted and I know where there's plenty that does," she announced sulkily. "And they pays for it!"

Alf caught her arm. Well, what the hell! It was done. Too bleeding late to change things.

He tucked her hand under his arm and sighed. She'd be anybody's for a pie and a jar, but for all that she was special to him . . .

James Grantly glanced back along the path, watched them walk swiftly away. He had actually been shocked by what he had seen. Not that such things were in the least unusual to him, swapping wives for a jar of ale was as rife in St Giles as the gentry taking a mistress in Bloomsbury. No, it was the fact that it was Alfred Hackett that had appalled him.

Yet, why should he be so surprised; the man had attacked Camilla, hadn't he? But that had been the drink and Alfred had seemed to keep sober for weeks now. He had believed that Alfred would never behave that way unless he was blind drunk. Well, it seemed he was wrong, for here he was in broad daylight linking arms with a woman who was all too obviously a street woman, and having the damned nerve to say she was a friend of Jenny's. He struck out with his cane at a blade of grass with annoyance, then sighed and pulled himself together. Why, in damnation did it matter to him anyway? He'd got the man a job for the third time and he'd helped Jenny make ends meet when things were bad. If Alfred couldn't behave himself after that . . . well . . . !

"Why, Doctor Grantly, what a surprise to find you taking the air in the gardens!"

He removed his hat swiftly and inclined his head. "My pleasure indeed, Mrs Germain, and such a beautiful evening, too. I trust you have enjoyed your free day?"

Mrs Germain smiled her most enchanting smile. "Indeed, I have." She was most relieved that he had been so pre-occupied with his thoughts that he had not noticed her tripping deftly across the lawns to contrive this 'surprise' meeting. She had followed him for half and hour, just awaiting such an opportunity as this. It was foolish, of course. She would see him at home, but there she was always the housekeeper in her wretched grey. She sought every opportunity that might enable him to see her dressed as she was today in colours that gave her more youth.

He replaced his hat and tucked his cane under his arm. "You will accompany me?" he asked, a little disappointed at having his solitude disturbed.

"Thank you, I will." She fell in step beside him. "Are not the gardens looking marvellous?" she purred.

He glanced around hurriedly. "Indeed, they are, ma'am, indeed, they are!"

"I am of the opinion that flowers give so much pleasure," she said with a long sigh. "Why I was talking to Miss Lees a few days ago and she told me that Miss Haddesley received a magnificent bouquet of flowers from a Mr Buchanan. Really beautiful she said it was. But then no doubt she will receive many more for I understand they are betrothed!"

James Grantly said nothing. His throat became suddenly dry and he felt a slight shiver vibrate through his body although the evening was still warm. So Camilla was betrothed! Yet she had given him no indication of it, indeed he had supposed her to find the man a nuisance. Well, he might have expected it, yet no, how could he have mistaken the looks she gave him, the delight when he said her name. He had always thought of her as Camilla since he had attended her brother-in-law.

Del Amberley was improving; Professor Lister had taken him into his nursing home. There would undoubtedly be a scar, but then he was lucky to be alive, lucky to have someone like Camilla for a sister-in-law.

Mrs Germain chatted on, accepting his short replies with the satisfaction of one who knows she has achieved what she set out to do. Then quite suddenly he changed. It was as if he came back into her world with a new zest. They talked about the park, about the profusion of trees to be found there, about the birds, then the subject of music seemed quite naturally to follow.

"You enjoy musical concerts, Mrs Germain?" he asked.

"Why, Doctor Grantly, you know I love them!"

He was suddenly over come by impulse, an unusual situation for James Grantly, he reached into his pocket and took out a card. "Then perhaps Mrs Germain, you would consider accompanying me to a piano recital at the home of a friend of mine." He held out the invitation. That he had intended to ask Camilla to go with him he tried unsuccessfully to forget.

Mrs Germain lifted her eyes to his with a purposeful slowness. "I would love to accept," she said simply.

He glanced away quickly, unable to meet her intense gaze. What on earth had possessed him to ask this creature to spend an evening with him? Didn't he see enough of her at home? A picture of Alfred flashed though his mind, Alfred with the woman in the gaudy pink dress. What a walk he had had tonight; first to find Alfred unashamedly unfaithful to Jenny . . . then to discover that

Camilla, whom he had begun to love, was betrothed to another man. And to end it all, here he was falling victim to the positively devious charms of his own housekeeper. And he had come this way for a peaceful walk . . .

On the following morning Camilla was busy at work. She had herself discovered two new cases of Erysipelis, and this added to the twenty in St Giles already being nursed. Chicken Pox had faded for a while as the warmer weather of spring heralded the summer to come. It was August; in another two days she would be applying for her certificate. Another year, she mused, and I shall be twenty-five.

She was glad that Robbie's little family seemed to be coping well enough. Dr Grently had kept a continual flow of errands moving Robbie's nimble feet. She had not seen the doctor today. Sometimes it was like that; their paths just didn't seem to cross. But still she was filled with a warm glow when she remembered their parting at Cleveland

Row, and his face was rarely far from her mind.

It was almost lunchtime when a somewhat humorous sight caught her eye; she could hardly believe it. What madness was this? A large unwieldy carriage was making its way down the deeply potholed street towards her, She stood transfixed staring at the oncoming carriage, then suddenly she realized that not only did she recognise the coachman, but Sir Walter's head was thrust out through the window. Camilla had thought he was in Scotland; when the London season had ended, he had packed his fishing rod and gun, and joined in the general migration northwards to the Scottish moors. Now, here he was back in London, and looking, it seemed, for Camilla.

She heard him shout: "There she is! Stop, confound it! Stop, do you hear me?"

Patiently she waited on the edge of the road whilst the horses were reined in, and the carriage creaked and groaned to a halt.

"Ah, there you are, Miss Haddesley," he sighed, opening the door and leaning out towards her.

She agreed that indeed here she was.

He indicated that she should climb inside, obviously having no intention of stepping down on to the cobblestones himself. She passed her bag up to him and then stepped agilely up into the carriage. The comfortable seat was, in fact, a great pleasure after a morning on her feet.

"I have come to thank you," he said simply, aware quite suddenly that gratitude was a sentiment that he rarely felt.

She turned her head in surprise.

"For saving Del's life," he augmented. "Alexander has given me all the details; I know I can never really repay you for what you have done."

She was amazed, that she had possibly saved Del's life she would not argue, but that anyone needed to repay her for such a deed was beyond her comprehension. Del, was, of course, an only son, having four sisters so she understood his importance to Sir Walter. But thanks?

"Del's recovery is sufficient thanks," she said simply.

He sat back on the seat, fingered his whiskers for a moment then smiled. "I thought you would think it so," he said mildly, "and therefore I decided to reward you in something you would not consider for yourself."

She waited, greatly intrigued. What could he mean?

"I will do whatever it is you want here in St Giles." Then he sighed with resignation as if he had got something very unpleasant off his chest.

If he had asked her to marry him, (he was a widower) she would not have been more surprised. She just stared at him, quite unable to voice the sheer joy that took hold of her body and mind. "The houses," she gasped at last, "you mean you will build new houses with drains and privies and . . . "

"It wasn't just repairs you wanted then?" he enquired somewhat soberly. "No . . . I might have known it wouldn't be so confoundedly simple." Then with a deep sigh he nodded his head. "I capitulate, new houses." He glanced around him. "This one street only, mind you. I declare that is enough!"

If she could have chosen the place, she would have named this very street.

"Make some notes of those ideas you have in that scheming mind of yours and I will set about buying the property. When the purchase is completed I'll get an architect on the job. These people will have to quit their homes, of course, but they can have first option on the new houses." He put in his monocle and peered at her closely. "Does that please you, ma'am? Will you be satisfied with one street or am I supposed to foot the bill for the whole damned parish?"

Tearfully she nodded, her cheeks

already damp. "That's wonderful!" she told him then she leaned over and kissed his cheek.

He tutted and moved away as if he were offended, but she could see that he was pleased with her small gesture of gratitude.

"Well, I'll be off," he barked suddenly. "I have a luncheon appointment at my club, and I dare say you have some more of this nursing thing to do."

She began to open the door, smiling down at a group of barefooted children who had gathered on the road.

"Send me those ideas," he grunted. "Can't promise to use them but I suppose you know as well as anybody what's wanted in this wretched place."

★ ★ ★

"Isn't it marvellous! We're actually fully-fledged district nurses at last," exclaimed Alice proudly, swinging her fair curls

For Camilla, thirty-five pounds a

year was no great amount, but she could manage quite nicely on it. Her pride still forbade her from using the accounts which Del had opened for her. Foolish pride perhaps, for the help was offered with love, yet still she was determined to be self-sufficient.

Both Alice and she were delighted to have single rooms now; Bloomsbury Square began to feel more and more like home. Alice was fortunate to have an allowance from her father which made things a great deal easier.

"I do wish they would start building those houses," Camilla said to Alice one day.

Alice shook her head. "You're too impatient, Camilla, these things take time."

Camilla sighed, then she sat tapping her fingers together at the tips; it was something she had a habit of doing when she was deep in thought. She had met James Grantly precisely five times today and every time there had been the same cool politeness. It had been like that for days now. Ever since his visit to Del, she supposed; she just could not understand it. He would talk to her but their discourse always seemed to be of work. The rapport between them had gone, and he avoided her eyes with alarming regularity. How her heart ached because of it. Why he had changed, she did not know. Perhaps she had been mistaken to believe she was of any particular importance to him. The pursuit game which had turned into love was ended. Perhaps after all, Mrs Germain had won!

On the following evening she accepted an invitation to spend the evening with Alexander. He sought her company often enough; she must try to count her blessings. Yet there seemed no ease between them; she felt forever on her guard, on her best behaviour. It was strange but it was only with Dr Grantly that she had experienced that intuitive unity of mind and spirit which she had thought to be love. How much she had to learn! How little she really knew of this thing called love!

August passed slowly for Camilla. She enjoyed many simple pleasures in the few hours of leisure allowed to her. Sometimes she and Alice would sit on the embankment in the evening watching the boats moving slowly up river on the ebbing tide. The red, sailing barges were her favourites; so colourful in the pale, evening sky.

Camilla had taken Alice with her to visit the architect for the houses, but he could reveal nothing of Sir Walter's plans. He was most kind and apologetic, and indeed Alice seemed quite taken by him.

September came and melted away. Sir Walter, who had been touring Europe returned to England, but it was Alfred Hackett who gave Camilla the first news of the change, and she was deeply hurt not to be the first to know.

"They're throwing us out, Nurse," he shouted after her when she was out on her visits. She realized at once that he was very drunk. He had been making such an effort, too, and had held down his job for months.

"Who is throwing you out?" she asked, turning round and walking back towards him. She was not afraid of him.

She had learned of the respect her uniform commanded; even Alfred's drink-fuddled mind knew the blue cloak of the Association.

He was unsteady, grasping like a child at the wall beside him, his hair awry, his eyes bloodshot. "The new bloody landlord," he growled, his speech slurred and showing signs of growing anger. "I'll kill 'im," he vowed, regaining his balance and stumbling towards her. "I'll kill 'im when I find out 'oo 'e is." He tossed back his head as if to clear his brain. Weren't there enough problems keeping a wife fed and clothed and keeping Mary sweet without losing his home?

Camilla moved slightly to the side, removing herself from his path. But as he came on, he seemed to become dizzy again; holding his arms out towards her; then suddenly he stumbled, fell to the ground and lay there sobbing like a child.

It was a sight she would never forget. She had seen him like this many a time, but never before had this man's despair been because of her.

She knelt down beside him on the cobblestones, putting a hand on his arm. "You are not being thrown out, Mr Hackett," she assured him. "They are building a new house for you. It will be much better, you will see."

He opened his eyes and stared up at her. "And where do we sleep till they're built?" he asked. "In the gutters?"

She lifted her eyes from his, let them roam over the street around her. Surely some arrangement had been made. Surely they didn't just throw people out into the street . . . yet . . . there were hundreds of families in this street; where could they possibly go?

With a sickening pain in her stomach

she knew the answer. Soon they would be joining those who wandered homelessly about the streets at night; those who slept under bridges or huddled in doorways for shelter from the bitter coldness of the night.

6

CAMILLA pulled her cloak more closely around her shoulders and shivered. November was always cold and this one was as bad as any. Her whole body was chilled by the damp fog. It hung everywhere, menacing and so quiet. She never knew such quiet as when the fog silenced streets like a huge, grey blanket.

As she walked on, figures passed her in the gloom; not speaking, nor caring who she was. Yet she would not complain; she and the other nurses were fortunate. They had a roof over their heads and a warm fire to return to. She turned her head to look back over the street, foolishly forgetting the fog. Well, she didn't need to see it to know it was dead. Empty courts, the houses pulled down into rubble and dust.

She walked on, hearing only the soft thud of her own footsteps. How relieved she had been when Alice had found Robbie's family a temporary home with a coachman that worked for her father. Jenny and Alfred, too, had been lucky because Jenny's sister had married a tanner in Whitechapel and had been able to take them in for a while. The children had been settled in a school, too.

When Camilla almost bumped into Jenny a moment later she was quite shocked. Never had she seen Jenny look so devastated. This woman had nursed Alf through illness, borne his drunkenness, listened to his raving about another woman, but always in the end he had come home. Today they had arrested him for theft. Without him she was lost.

"'e ain't never took nothing before, Nurse," she pleaded, doubts of his innocence increasing. "It was the drink, I expect." She paused to wipe her tearstained face with her sleeve. Then she went on, half sobbing, half talking. "But that won't make no difference — they won't listen to me. Ten years they'll give 'im and it'll kill 'im, sure as tea is tea."

Camilla knew Jenny believed what she said, but in truth how many other times had there been? Dr Grantly's omission to name Alfred when he had attacked her was the thing that was troubling her now. She herself could think of nothing to do, but what of James Grantly? What reason could there be for him to protect a man such as Alfred Hackett?

"Does Dr Grantly know?" she asked Jenny gently.

Jenny shook her head. "Shouldn't think so, I ain't told no one 'cept you. But I can't ask 'im to do nothin', Nurse Haddesley. He's been so good, findin' Alf them jobs and givin' me that money and everything."

Camilla's eyebrows shot up with surprise. "He gave you money?" she asked.

Jenny looked guilty. "Well, yes, but you won't tell no one will you, Nurse. It was after I was ill, like. 'e give me money for food, a little each week. But I couldn't ask 'im to do no more."

"You don't have to," Camilla said. "But I think he would like you to tell him about Alf being in prison . . . yes, he would expect you to tell him about that." How she wished she could tell him herself but their relationship had not improved at all. He was curt to the point of rudeness with her now.

Jenny thanked Camilla wearily, still knowing nothing but despair, then she set off hurriedly down Bedford Place towards the doctor's house.

The next Camilla knew of the matter was when she actually saw Alf Hackett, large as life, walking towards Picadilly Circus. And only three days had passed. She sought out Jenny at the first opportunity. The lady, it seemed had withdrawn the charge, saying she was mistaken; she had dropped her purse and Alfred had kindly picked it up for her. It sounded rather farfetched to Camilla. Jenny put her own thoughts into words.

"I reckon it's the doctor," she said. "I told 'im like you said. He won't admit to nothin' though, but I reckon it was 'im got my Alf free."

How curious, Camilla mused. What reason could Dr Grantly have for going to such lengths to help this particular man?

Jenny seemed completely changed by Alf's release. There was a new fire in her eyes that had been missing for some time. What Camilla did not know was that Jenny had decided that it was time she won back her husband from Mary Ware.

For weeks the houses had lain in rubble. Now the area had been cleared; at last buildings were going up. Clouds of dust mingled with another day of fog, choking the still, damp air. Camilla stood watching, one day in the middle of December.

"They'll be smashin' when they're

done, Nurse" a familiar voice said beside her.

She smiled with pleasure as Robbie Gower moved quickly to her side. "Yes, Robbie, but they are taking a good deal of time. I'm sure you will be one of the first though." That was rash; she knew it at once.

"You mean we'll get an 'ouse!" he gasped, with obvious astonishment. Robbie never expected anything; therefore was rarely disappointed.

She laughed. "Well, I don't suppose you will get one all to yourself, but I am sure they will find you a room somewhere."

He beamed, his pinched face really glowed with pure delight. Any efforts Camilla made for his benefit were in that smile repaid.

In the dimness of the fog, a dark shadow moved. She could not say who it was, but Camilla made out the shape of a man as he walked away. There was a slight uneasiness in his gait, indicative of a limp, she thought. For a moment she considered calling him back. Had he perhaps wanted her? But no, he was gone, dissolved into the fog.

She left Robbie still watching the builders and continued on her calls. On the next street she all but collided with Dr Grantly.

"Why, Miss Haddesley" he exclaimed, removing his hat. "The very person I was hoping to see!"

She felt the warmth of colour rising to her cheeks and dropped her eyes but he must have seen it. "You have a message for me?" she enquired assuming his words to be related to work. She had spoken quite calmly but how her heart thudded! Would she never be rid of this aching, this longing to be near him? Their meetings now seemed almost purposely cut short, yet before she could have sworn there were times when he seemed to linger in her company. And that hope he had expressed of using her first name; yet since that night he had never done so. Well, she supposed people changed, but why, oh why, this man she loved?

Suddenly she noticed that his necktie was awry; at once she wanted to put out her hand and straighten it. He looked well, this morning, yet, as her eyes unwittingly searched his handsome face she saw the lines again, the signs of care, of encountered pain and she knew in that moment that somewhere in James Grantly's life there was a sadness, a deep personal tragedy. And not, as she had supposed before, just the deep compassion he had for his patients. She wondered then what harsh blow had been dealt this man. If Mrs Germain were now an important part of his life, and she had seen them walking together many times, then she was not, as Camilla would have forecast, making him any happier than before.

He smiled at her now, but it was the tight little smile of politeness where once there had been that pleasant lop-sided grin. "Why, not a message exactly; in fact, I am a little uncertain how to put it. But in view of what you told me some months ago, I rather feel that you have something to do with this rebuilding programme. May I ask, am I right in this assumption?"

Camilla sighed lightly, only Alice and she knew of her involvement and she did not wish it to be known further. "You are, Dr Grantly, Sir Walter is responsible for financing the new housing." Impulsively she smiled up at him. How she longed to melt that cold exterior, to banish the severe mask he had donned, for somehow she felt sure now that it was a mask. What of her pride? Well, there are perhaps times when one's pride must be thrust aside; suddenly she was eager to grasp any chance whatsoever of propelling herself into his company. "I would be most grateful if you would keep this information to yourself" she entreated him.

"By all means, Miss Haddesley, by all means! I will, of course, respect your wishes. I had, however, a rather personal reason for determining the new landlord." He hesitated and raised his dark eyebrows in question. "Can you spare me a moment more?" he asked.

"Why, of course, Dr Grantly," she replied, quite unconsciously straightening her bonnet.

He went on: "It has occurred to me that it might be of great value to the people here if I could open a dispensary in this area; a place where they could come at a fixed time each day. I wondered, if fact, if there might be any possibility of my renting one of the new houses for this purpose. I could perhaps let the upper floor, as I would only require two rooms downstairs — " He broke off, and looked intently down into her eyes.

"I would greatly value your opinion on the matter, Miss Haddesley."

She glanced away, unable to bear his gaze any longer, then she replied quite calmly, "Why it seems a highly commendable idea, Dr Grantly, but you would, of course, be making a

155

great deal of work for yourself."

He nodded in agreement. "But the prevention of disease, my dear Miss Haddesley, must surely be worth the effort. I am certain that is one thing on which we both agree."

"Why, of course, and were you wishing me to bring the matter up with Sir Walter?"

"It would be most kind of you," he replied, then he smiled quite openly this time and her heart lurched most painfully. "I trust you enjoyed your evening at the Savoy last night," he asked, his eyes searching her face.

"Why, yes," she stammered, supposing someone had told him of her evening there with Alexander.

"I was there myself," he explained, "with my house-keeper Mrs Germain. I met Mr Buchanan in the foyer. Perhaps he mentioned it?"

She shook her head, Alexander had said nothing. So Mrs Germain had won!

"Ah, well, no. He was telling me how

proud he was of the work you do. I was, of course delighted to hear of your betrothal . . . I understand that we may be soon losing you from Bloomsbury Square. I . . . I just wanted to say that I wish you every happiness."

Camilla was shocked, so shocked that for a moment she was quite speechless. Then she blinked her eyes and pulled herself together. "I assure you Dr Grantly that I have no plans for leaving Bloomsbury Square, and if Mr Buchanan has led you to believe that we are betrothed then he is very much mistaken. I . . . I shall of course put your request to Sir Walter. I suspect his only concern will be that the rents be paid."

There was a flickering in his dark eyes, a light that came suddenly as she spoke, and she found herself once more held fast by his dark-eyed gaze. "You are not betrothed?" he said, then, as if collecting his thoughts, "I would be most grateful," his voice hardened as if he had to swallow — "then I would be most grateful if you would approach Sir Walter for me. And believe me, Miss Haddesley, I am quite delighted to hear that you are not thinking of leaving us. Now, I bid you a very good morning. I have already taken up too much of your time."

Camilla returned the greeting half dazed by his words. But who had told him she was betrothed to Alexander? Surely Alexander would not have taken a liberty like that. But Mrs Germain might stoop so low as to tell such a lie. Camilla turned angrily away and continued into the court where she was bound. In the shadows a man stood watching, a man she did not know, and when he moved away there was the uneven thud of one boot and the following tap of his wooden stump.

★ ★ ★

It was the evening before Christmas Eve. Alice and Camilla were in Covent Garden to buy holly to decorate the drawing room at the Home. Camilla was in a most cheerful mood. Her changed relationship with James Grantly gave new joys almost every day. They had once again become at ease with each other, although as yet those meetings were still confined to those at work.

"I do wish he would ask you to dine again," Alice sighed. "I am quite on edge about it all."

Camilla laughed lightly. "One would think it was you who craved his attention, not I! Why the poor man has been rushed off his feet these last weeks. No, I am content. He is not an impetuous man and I know now that at least I can be hopeful."

"Which, my dear, is more than I can say for myself. Not a man in sight and I am fast becoming an old maid."

Camilla clicked her tongue with disgust. "What nonsense, Alice! You are younger then I. And if you must be so choosy then you must expect to wait a little for the gentleman who pleases you. Why, you have had three offers and I only one. And that so many years ago I scarce remember what he said." Then she laughed again. "We have holly to buy and there are ears in this place that are, I'll declare, quite as large as any donkey's."

Alice laughed and nodded her agreement readily. How they both loved the Garden at Christmas. All around them lay the prickly, red-berried bundles, and the dull green masses of mistletoe with its clusters of creamy white dots. Donkey carts laden high with green upon green, wending their way towards the large houses and hotels. Wagons ambling along through the market, loaded with Christmas trees to be decked with tinsel and presents galore.

Everywhere was so colourful; The brilliant orange, yellow and gold of the fruit; masses and masses of flowers; chrysanthemums of every shade, making the most of their seasonal abundance, filling the air with their delicate fragrance. And another smell, warm and pleasant, of chestnuts roasting on an open fire. The usual decline in trade at this hour of day was not in evidence; the garden simply bustled with people and echoed with vibrant noise. The trade of these days before Christmas would have to keep the costers in the lean months to come.

For the last week, Camilla had watched the great flocks of geese being herded through the town on their way to Smithfield Market, but she doubted any of the people of St Giles would be tasting goose for their Christmas dinner. Even beef and mutton which sold for around four pence a pound in the summer were raised to one shilling or more in the winter. A few families with hens might manage to kill a bird for their dinner; some might even have a share in a pig, but most would be satisfied with a halfpenny worth of stewed eels or a crust of bread in their vegetable broth.

"They've started taking names for

them 'ouses, Nurse," a rough, croaking voice reached Camilla suddenly from behind a six foot fir.

"They have?" she gasped. "Are they to move in yet?"

Bessie Lewis clambered with great difficulty between her trees, shouting their merits loudly across the street as she did so. Then she dropped her voice and leaned closer to Alice and Camilla. "I 'eard they was giving keys out this week," she got out quickly, before resuming her raucous cry. Then she added; "They've got a list, special people what's to be offered them 'ouses. Don't seem right that. Shameful I'd call it."

At last they were allocating the houses. Camilla said: "I don't think that's quite true, Bessie. I believe the people whose houses had been demolished are to have first choice. That seems fair don't you think?" How wary she must be of saying too much.

"Now then, lovely tree, sir," Bessie

162

cooed. "Look a treat with silver tinsel and them red balls and the like. Thank you, sir. Taking it now are you?" She pocketed the coins and heaved the largest of the trees across to the top hatted gentleman who now seemed unsure whether to hold it high in the air or tuck it under his arm. In the end he dragged it behind him, looking very self-conscious as if he were afraid he might be recognized.

"I wonder if he's taking it on the train?" Alice giggled.

"Not 'im, dearie," Bessie growled in their ears, as she rubbed an apple on her somewhat grubby apron. "He lives in Bloomsbury. Curator fella at that Museum place near you."

Alice laughed. "One of our neighbours then."

Bessie scowled suddenly, then bit deeply into the apple. "And 'ere comes one of mine. Watch out for your purses, ladies!" This last comment was breathed hoarsely through a mouthful of peel.

They turned to see Mrs Dawson Robbie's ex-landlady, coming towards them, her grey bonnet pulled tightly around her face; a large grey shawl around her huddled shoulders and covered by an even larger one of dark green which reached almost to her knees. She wore no gloves and Camilla thought how odd it was that a woman who spent her day making them should have none for herself. Her face, pinched by the cold weather seemed dominated more than ever by her long, pointed nose.

"I 'ear Nellie Bird's got a key then," she rattled out pointedly at Bessie, ignoring the two district nurses but speaking loud enough for them to hear.

"So she says," Bessie offered vaguely, showing little interest and busying herself in arranging mistletoe which did not need arranging.

Mrs Dawson gave one of her best sniffs. "Shouldn't wonder if them brats what lived with me don't get an 'ouse.

And me and Dawson with nothing but a lodging 'ouse roof over our 'eads."

"You will have the same chance as every body else, Mrs Dawson," Camilla put in hurriedly, unable to hold her tongue any longer.

"And 'ow would you know then, Nurse? Something to do with you, is it?" she demanded tauntingly, relaxing her hold on her shawl so that it just slipped off her shoulder and revealed to Camilla's astonishment what appeared to be an emerald brooch.

"No, of course not," she returned angrily. "We have just heard those details from the agent, haven't we, Nurse Kilbride?"

Alice agreed readily, walking away as if she had had enough.

Mrs Dawson tugged the shawls back swiftly, pulling them tightly around her shoulders, and wrapping her hands in the folds. Then she sniffed again and pushed her pointed nose so close to Camilla that she was forced to turn away to escape the foul-smelling breath.

"Your fancy man?" she asked, baring her black teeth in a supercilious smile, her voice high-pitched and mocking.

Camilla flushed with anger. "What can you mean?" she demanded.

"Don't you get haughty with me, miss. I seen you, getting into a fine carriage with a gentleman twice your age." She lifted her head, pulled back her shoulders in an effort to gain height. "Give 'im a kiss, she did, Bessie, and 'er all smiles after the doctor an' all."

Camilla was visibly enraged. She was absolutely furious. She could only suppose the woman was referring to her meeting with Sir Walter; the remark about James Grantly she tried to ignore. For a moment she could think of nothing else but hitting the woman on the head with the holly they had just bought. She raised her arm to strike. This, and the redness of her face caused Mrs Dawson to back away from her rapidly, her own beady eyes wide and staring.

166

Alice caught her friend's arm and all but dragged her away. "Come along, Camilla," she begged. "We have more important things to do than to listen to stupid women who don't know what they are talking about."

Camilla calmed down at once. How glad she was that Robbie was no longer under Mrs Dawson's roof. She supposed that woman had not forgiven her for interfering in her infant labour. But under whose roof Robbie would live was still a problem; if the keys were indeed being handed out then she must make some effort to accommodate the children somewhere. Without Mrs Dawson's knowledge, of course.

It was whilst they were festooning the drawing room later that day, that young Joe, Robbie Gower's brother arrived, shivering with cold and clad only in his shirt and trousers. After telling them that Robbie was: "all bleedin' and keepin' on bawlin'," he was taken down to the kitchen at Miss

Lees' instructions to be clothed more warmly and fed with hot broth.

Alice and Camilla set off in a cab to Bethnal Green to the home of Alice's father's coachman.

That Robbie had been climbing chimneys was obvious at once. He lay on the bed, his face stained with tears, the sheets stained with blood and very black. The coachman's wife knew nothing of the affair.

"I ain't cryin' cause o' the pain, you know. It's just 'cause I wanted to get a room in one o' them houses and Dawson said we'd 'ave to pay three shillin' for a room."

That Mrs Dawson's husband was involved Camilla might have guessed. She was absolutely furious. He was obviously spreading ridiculous rumours and this sweep was a friend of his, too. By the time Alice and Camilla left, Robbie was much more comfortable and Camilla had calmed down a little. She determined to sort out Dawson, however; sending children up chimneys like that was against the law quite apart from anything else.

As they had sent the cab away, they began to walk back towards the town, intending to find another hansom. Camilla had never in fact seen Dawson although his wife crossed her path often enough. The man seemed determined to interfere with young Robbie.

"Listen!" said Alice suddenly. "Listen!"

Camilla stood quite still and listened, then she, too, heard the joyful singing. They had crossed The Haymarket and were walking down the Whitechapel Road. "How lovely!" she exclaimed. "How happy they sound!"

Soon they came to an open doorway. A crowd gathered in the street, blocking the way. The volume of the singing was really loud now; it filled the whole area with an eager, joyous hymn. Very slowly the people in the street were making their way inside, being welcomed at the door by two men in navy-blue fisherman's jerseys with an embroidered motif on the chest.

Carefully Camilla and Alice man-oeuvred a path through and were about to continue on their way when they heard a voice calling Camilla by name, and strangely, a voice so changed that she scarcely recognised it.

Then Alfred Hackett came towards her, smiling as she had never seen him smile before. Even in the light from the lantern by the doorway she could see that his whole appearance was altered, too. No longer was he the stooping, pathetic man whose moods were up and down like a see-saw. Here was a straight-backed man, confident, glowing with warmth and with a clearness in his eyes that was startling. His hair was now neatly combed, his suit well brushed, his face spotless and shaven.

"I'm really glad to see you Nurses," he said. "I've some wonderful news to tell you. I've found the Lord!"

A moment later, Jenny was by his side. He turned to look down at her and smiled into her eyes.

She moved closer to him and laid her hand on his shoulder. "It's true, Nurse 'addesley," she said softly. "It's really true!"

Nurse 'addesley," she said softly. "It's

7

AS Camilla was walking down Oxford Street she saw Jenny on the other side of the road. Surprisingly, Jenny was loaded with parcels, which she almost dropped in an effort to raise her hand.

"Got one of those 'ouses, Nurse 'addesley!" she shouted.

Camilla darted between the carts and cabs, and joined Jenny with a sigh of relief. "Marvellous!" she exclaimed.

"And Alf's got a new job!" Jenny beamed, her eyes shining.

"'es been given a job in printin'. Evenin' Standard it is they do. And it means that when 'e's learned a bit more about it 'e can 'elp with the printin' at the Mission, an' all. You know, the Salvationist, the Army's paper." She tilted her head on one side challengingly. "What do you think of that then?"

172

"Why that's marvellous!" Camilla exclaimed, adding the exuberance that was obviously expected of her, and making a mental note to buy a copy of the Salvationist.

"The pay's not a lot yet," Jenny confided quietly, "but it'll be regular and enough to pay the rent on the new house. With the little bit I get from the market we'll do quite nicely."

Camilla had an idea. "I wonder, Jenny, would you consider taking a lodger?"

"Someone for you, dear, of course I would."

Camilla frowned thoughtfully. "Well, it's not exactly a lodger," she explained. "it's the Gower family. You know, Robbie, Joe, Rose and Amy." She waited, but Jenny was thinking. "They could pay the rent and they manage very well on their own. It's just that . . . well, I was hoping to find a good family where they could lodge and you and Alf would be perfect. After that Mrs Dawson I feel they deserve a better chance."

Jenny smiled, a beautiful, understanding smile. "Then what can I say, Nurse. You've been so good to us."

A few drops of rain splattered down on the pavement, and Jenny jumped. "My, I must get these things inside or Alf'll never forgive me." Then she laughed out loud. "Why, what will I say next? And 'im the most forgiving man in this world."

Together they set off towards St Giles. For Camilla there was a busy afternoon ahead. When they heard the gentle hub-hub of voices in the distance they thought nothing of it, but when they reached the new houses they both realised that it came from quite a sizeable crowd. Camilla, a little ahead of Jenny, turned the corner and came face to face with a sea of hostility.

"There she is!" a man cried out. And the people turned towards her, silent, staring, menacing.

"That's the one," shouted another, waving his arm.

Camilla just could not believe it. She stood motionless, frozen to the spot, staring dumbfoundedly at the mass of faces. The warmth drained from her cheeks, her hands began to tremble a little. What did it mean? She could imagine no reason why she should be the object of such visible hate. She opened her mouth to speak, but no words came; her mouth was too dry with fear.

In front of her, some thirty yards away stood men and women from St Giles. Children ragged and barefoot; women clutching thin shawls around their bent shoulders. Their angry menfolk banded together on one side. And their faces — never would she forget their faces; every one twisted and lined with hate.

"Best run, Nurse," Jennie's trembling voice said behind her, but like a nightmare Camilla knew only too well that she could not run. Her joints were locked; muscles frozen with terror. Like a statue of stone with only eyes that moved she was rigid with fear. Her eyes darted from face to face; her mind disbelieving what she saw.

Then suddenly, she could move; she began to turn, to run, but as she did so the mob moved forward, closing in around her, shouting, jeering as they came. These people she had loved and cared for, had her pinned against the wall of a newly-built brick house.

"She's the one stopped us gettin' 'ouses" she heard to her amazement. "Got 'er own friends in, that's for sure."

She glanced about looking for Jenny but she was nowhere to be seen. What she did notice was a man with a wooden leg and somehow she knew he was the man she had seen in the shadows when she was with young Robbie. Now, he came struggling through and they let him pass until he stood face to face with her. His matted hair was long, his unshaven face a picture of gloating pleasure. And unlike the rest of them, his eyes were alight; wild with excitement, brilliant with a strange look of madness.

"I 'eard you," he accused, raising his voice as if they were on the stage and he the star player. "Told the doctor she'd get 'im an 'ouse, she did. And that brat Robbie Gower, promised 'im a room an' all, and — "

"Stop it, stop it," she cried, finding her voice at last, anger displacing fear. "I had no say in who was given houses and who was not. You all had equal opportunity."

The jeering began again. She tried to shout above it but her voice was drowned by the raucous noise.

"You tell her, Dawson," someone shouted. She stared at the man to whom the words were directed. Dawson; Dawson! The man with the stump was Dawson.

Something hit her on the arm and rattled down on to the ground. Then another, and another. She realised with horrifying alarm that they were throwing stones. She looked around her with terror but could see no escape. Perspiration ran down her face. Behind her was a solid wall, all around her were accusing eyes and flying stones. One hit her on the head; when she touched it, there was blood.

"Stop it!" she cried. "Please stop it" In vain she tried to shout again, to beg them to think what they were doing. But still the stones came, and the laughs, the shouts and the coarse remarks. She could almost feel the hostility, the very air seemed filled with loathing. She turned her face away, tried to fend off the flying stones.

Suddenly, a voice rose above the shouts. A last stone clattered short on the cobbles below. It was a strangely commanding voice, raised as she, only once, had heard it before. She fell to the ground from relief, from exhaustion, and crouched there like a cornered animal.

A tall figure thrust his way through the crowd, and behind him was Jenny, tears streaming down her face. Jenny minus the precious parcels. Then James spoke again:

"What are you doing?" he asked them, pushing his way towards Camilla, starting when he saw her on the ground then lifting her to her feet in the circle of his arms. At once she felt safe; felt the warmth of his body coming through to her own.

"What madness is this?" he demanded, staring around him at the shuffling eyeless crowd. "You're hurt," he said to Camilla in a whisper. "My God, when Jenny told me what they were doing!"

She had no time to answer; a loud voice took his eyes from her face. "You're all right! You're not out in the street! She put you on 'er list. You've got one bleedin' 'ouse already and you wanted another. Greedy bastard, that's what you are! Not the rest of us; she'll let us rot in the gutter."

For a brief second the man who shielded her with his own body looked down into her eyes. "There's no truth in that is there? You didn't make a list?"

She shook her head, trembling a little in his arms. "The dispensary house for you was the only one I mentioned to Sir Walter. Why, I only just heard about Jenny and Alf."

His eyes smiled at her but his face remained solemn. Then he turned back to the crowd and repeated what she had said, explaining to them what the dispensary house was for.

Many began mumbling amongst themselves, some started moving away. Then Jenny's voice came suddenly across to Camilla. It was shaking a little.

"You all leaving without a word, then," she challenged them. "You expect Nurse 'addesley to come back tomorrow, do you? Look after your children, no doubt, and pretend it didn't 'appen. Ain't there none of you got the courage to beg 'er forgiveness for what you've done. I bet there's no one 'ere who don't know someone who's been looked after by these nurses. There's me for a start!"

Feet shuffled. No one answered. Then a woman at the side leaned forward and pointed at Camilla. "She were the one who nursed my Jack afor 'e died. I reckon she ain't all that bad." Then another, and another. Slowly, admissions were dragged out of those men and women.

One by one they came, lowering their eyes and muttering words she could not hear; but they came. Dawson tried shouting again, stirring up a few to grumble as they went. But soon they were all gone; only a group of children playing five stones on the pavement were left.

James threw a coin towards them. "Get a cab!!" he shouted. A boy ran off down the street.

On the couch in James Grantly's study Camilla lay back and sighed. He had insisted on bringing her there, refusing to take her to the Home. She had almost slipped when getting out of the cab and he had gathered her up in his arms and carried her to the house.

Anger still lingered in his eyes now and still the tight-lipped firmness of his mouth. His coat was marked with dirt and she realised that he, too, must have been hit by flying stones.

Mrs Germain could scarcely believe this turn of events. She had been furious to discover the nurse to be none other than Miss Haddesley. She could almost believe the incident to be contrived but she had to admit the cuts and bruises looked genuine enough. She brought in hot water and Dr Grantly washed them himself.

"How could they," he breathed stormily. "How could they do this? What madness seized them?" It seemed that now the situation was in hand, the anger that had built up inside him, needed a vent.

As for Camilla, she was completely exhausted, quite unable to exert any kind of energy. A cup of strong coffee from Mrs Germain made her feel much better.

James checked her pulse for about the fifth time, examining her cuts very closely. "I shall need to put about six sutures in your head," he told her gently, adding; "Should I summon Miss Lees?"

She begged him not to do so. She did not feel very brave, but she trusted him. When the work was done she lay for a while with the curtains drawn, resting on cushions and a little dazed by the ether. After a while she slept.

When she awoke, he was sitting on a chair beside her, making a pretence of reading a book.

"I have visited Miss Lees," he told her softly. "She agrees that you must remain here for tonight. The guest room is ready whenever you feel you could manage the stairs." He peered at her a little closer, then smiled.

She began to sit up, the strangeness of the situation becoming more clear in her mind. She was quite over-whelmed with embarrassment. How often she had longed to visit this house; to see inside that black painted door. Now here she was, but in a position that no one could envy, all done up in bandages. Swiftly her eyes took in the shape and colour of the room. One whole wall was filled by well stocked bookshelves; a baby grand piano stood by the window. Did he play? she wondered. For no conceivable reason she suddenly thought of Mrs Germain. She lived in this house. Did she ever relax in this room or were her days really confined to the housekeeper's quarters?

"I shall give you something a little later to help you sleep," he was saying. "Could you manage a little tea perhaps? Mrs Germain makes excellent fruit cake."

They had tea together, James and Camilla. Camilla on the sofa and he at a small table set beside her. It was a pleasant meal apart from the aches and pains which she tried hard to put from her mind. They talked on a variety of subjects not touching their work. It struck Camilla again how in tune they were. The only cloud in the sky was the one which crossed the housekeeper's face when she was told that Camilla was to stay. Had she to begin all over again?

Mrs Germain was a servant, yet there was always an air of authority about her. She wore a dark grey dress which was trimmed with a starched white collar and cuffs. A lace cap sat rather pertly on her head. Her manner appeared kind, her voice soft, yet there was no warmth in it, at least for Camilla. And when she smiled it did not reach her clear, black eyes. Mrs Germain, Camilla concluded, was pleased to serve her when her employer could see it. Alone together, she showed a coldness which Camilla did not like. Her conversation became curt to the point of impoliteness.

James Grantly, however was kindness itself and his housekeeper's hostility was soon thrust to the back of Camilla's mind.

"I owe you a dinner," he said suddenly when they were alone. "I have never asked you again since your brother-in-law's accident."

She protested emphatically. "It was I who was unable to fulfil our engagement."

He folded his hands on his lap and looked her straight in the eye. How she wished then that she did not have a bandage on her head. "I refrained from asking you again because I believed you to be . . . betrothed to Mr Buchanan." He leaned forward a little, an eagerness in his voice, which was reflected by the brightness of his eyes. "But you are quite free from any obligation to him . . . or to any other man?"

"Why yes," she gasped, a little flustered by the directness of his questioning. "There is no one at all." She did not add, except for you.

"Then I am very glad of it, for I can ask you to dine with me; I mean, of course, when you feel well enough. Will you do me that honour, Miss Haddesley?"

She smiled, lowering her eyes with suitable humility. "I would be delighted to accept, Dr Grantly," she replied quietly, barely able to conceal her excitement.

"I assure you, the pleasure, my dear Miss Haddesley will be mine. And I will admit that I hope that our evening together will be one of many." He sat back in his chair, his head slightly tilted to one side. "Does that shock you Miss Haddesley? Does it offend you that I should be so blunt?"

She lifted her eyes to his and saw the light that shone from them. No, she wasn't dreaming; he really was talking to her. For a full thirty seconds she saw nothing in that room but his dark, compelling eyes. Then she spoke, almost in a whisper. "No, it does not shock me, Dr Grantly; in truth it pleases me."

Impulsively he leaned forward, taking

her hand in his. "I'm so very glad to hear you say that, so very glad!"

Then just as quickly his mood changed. He released her hand and got swiftly to his feet. "You must rest," he said sharply. "And I have some more calls to make." He crossed to his desk and turned over some papers. "And that reminds me, I have not thanked you for acquiring the house for me. I received a letter only this morning to confirm that I had been awarded number Thirty-Six. A most suitable choice, it is an end property."

All at once Camilla was reminded of her afternoon's ordeal. Tears flooded down her cheeks and she sat there sobbing uncontrollably. He was at her side immediately, wiping the tears away, cursing himself for having been so thoughtless. Between sobs she told him about Dawson, about the chimney sweeping business. It seemed better to talk about it now.

He sighed, holding her hand in his again. "And, of course, you do not wish it to be known that that it is to you they owe the fact that they have new houses at all."

She shook her head. "It is better that way."

"I will deal with Dawson," he said passionately. "There have been several instances lately in which he has been involved. There is enough evidence to have him thrown into prison for ten years. I see now that I have been neglectful in not reporting them to the police before. I thought to give him a chance, but no, I was wrong. He must be removed to where he can do no more harm."

She blew her nose and wiped away the rest of her tears. "He is so bitter. And it is true that many are made homeless by the building of new houses, but it really could not be helped."

"You will have no cause to worry your head about this at all, my dear. I will see the sergeant myself and do all that is necessary." He looked at her with sudden concern in his eyes. "This will not change your decision to stay at Bloomsbury?" he asked. "You will not consider leaving nursing because of it?"

She smiled up at him and shook her head slowly. Bruised and hurt though she was, she could have told him that nothing on earth would make her leave Bloomsbury Square now. Nothing would make her miss those evenings of which he had talked so openly.

8

"RIGHT now, come on, Camilla Haddesley! What's this between you and Dr Grantly?" Alice wasted no time in her question once the doctor was out of earshot. It was Camilla's first day back at work after her injury.

Camilla laughed. "What do you mean, Alice! Surely you can see it is just a little addition to our work."

Alice pulled her cloak more tightly around her shoulders. February had brought snow and when they had awoken that morning the square had been covered in white icing. They had seen the greyness of the sky, the slightly pink tint of the evening and felt the cold wind blowing from the north. "Why, I do declare you think I am an idiot, Camilla. That man is in love with you and you try to pretend you do not know it!"

Camilla took out her handkerchief and blew her nose in an effort to hide the pink colour of her cheeks.

"Oh, Alice," she exclaimed, "you are quite mistaken. What on earth could have given you such an idea?"

"The way he looked at you, my dear, the way he gazed into your eyes." She turned her head and seeing her friend's face she gave a laugh. "And your face Camilla, is really quite red. Now tell me do. What did he say to you when you spent the whole night at his house?"

In a way it was good to laugh; the morning had been full of misery; finding children dead from the cold and everyone shivering over small fires made of market boxes or sometimes even their own furniture.

Now Camilla was silent, she knew it was no use trying to hide the facts from her friend. At least if she told the truth, which after all was little more than a dinner invitation, then at least Alice would not create more in her imagination. When they had met James today it had been most awkward. They had seen him several times before that morning and Camilla knew with a warm glow of pleasure that he had been making himself available in case of trouble. The people of St Giles had been obviously repentant, calling the incident shocking, and some hiding the fact that they had actually been there. Dawson had been arrested.

James had greeted them as usual and they had told him of the miserable cases they had found. "I was wondering," he said, "if the Salvation Army could do anything about the fuel problem. Perhaps we could ask Mr Hackett."

Camilla agreed and Alice nodded her head.

He had glanced at Alice with doubt in his eyes, then made up his mind to continue. "I was considering going to Whitechapel this evening, Miss Haddesley. I wonder whether you would accompany me to give your opinion on the matter. Unless, of course, you feel it too much today?"

For a horrible moment Camilla had though Alice was about to offer to go. Her lips moved but no sound came out.

Camilla could see that Alice was unsure of the situation so she accepted the invitation and agreed a time for their meeting. Now, a short while later, she told Alice more about her stay at the doctor's house.

"Well, Camilla, I'm delighted!" Alice exclaimed. "And you are to join him tonight. What fun!"

"I would scarcely describe the purpose of our visit, fun, Alice," Camilla chided her.

Alice clasped her hands together and frowned dutifully.

"No, indeed not, but you will be alone with him on the journey, and, my dear, who knows what might become of that!"

Camilla laughed lightly. "You consider

then that I am quite at risk in his company?" she suggested.

Alice pursed her lips. "You know well enough, Camilla, that is not what I meant at all. And by the way, my dear, I have decided that my father is right," she added unexpectedly. "I shall throw myself into society as he wished, and make more effort to find a husband. When work permits, of course." She smiled a little wryly. "After all, Dr Grantly is only a poor doctor. I could make a much better catch for myself!"

Camilla laughed. How right she was, yet it caused her no concern at all. For her, life was blossoming, she could wish for nothing less for Alice.

The evening could not come soon enough. Once outside, and sure that several pairs of eyes were watching her, she climbed self-consciously up into the hansom. She did not see the figure who passed by on the causeway.

Mrs Germain kept well in the shadows as she made her way back to Russell Square. Her face was set grimly, hard lines ageing the usually smooth brow, the dark eyes cold as steel. So her worst fears were being realised. Already James was escorting Miss Haddesley. He had told her he was going to some mission place, which was obviously quite untrue. She must beware that he suspected her now, but action was called for, immediate action, and whatever happened he must not have the slightest reason to lay the blame at her door.

When they were settled in the cab James said: "It is really dishonest of me to ask you here tonight, for although your added testimony will give weight to my request, I must confess that my real reason for asking you was to have the pleasure of your company."

She smiled at him. "Then I can scarcely complain, for whilst our journey is indeed most important, I must own to the same reason for accepting."

He laughed, and she caught his laughter. "How glad I am," he sighed, "that we can be so honest with each other. I do so hate coyness and obscurity, don't you?"

She agreed that she did and sank happily back on to the cushion of the seat. Mrs Germain was very far from her mind.

At the Whitechapel People's Mission they were referred to a Captain Blandy, whom they found in 'The Shelter', a large room along which were ranged wooden boxes, each just big enough for the human body. Most of them were occupied, but still a line of men and women waited in the aisles in the hope of finding one empty.

Within minutes of their arrival James was tending the sick with Camilla's help. The fuel they wanted took second place.

They worked there for the whole evening, returning on the following one, too. Captain Blandy was overjoyed. He told them that he had that very morning been praying for medical help. Camilla thought hard about the coal, about the logs, then suddenly she knew what she could do. Her pride had forbidden her using the accounts at the city shops, but Del would never refuse her request to have a small personal allowance in the bank. She sent him a cable, receiving an answer the following morning. Then, finding a reliable coal merchant in the area, she placed an order for the next twenty weeks.

Captain Blandy was surprised to see them on the third evening. "If coal and logs were delivered to the Mission, could you distribute them?" she enquired.

"I have enough people to distribute anything, it's the goods that are in short supply," he replied with delight.

It was decided that those receiving coal and logs should pay for them. Not a large amount, nothing like the true value, but in this way they would not regard it as a free gift, or their right. The money obtained in this way was to be used for medicine for the Mission.

A week later James found Camilla

with Mrs Gantry. The poor woman had an infected ulcer on her leg. She could hardly walk, and the treatment seemed of little help.

"And how is the leg progressing?" he asked politely.

"Not too well, Doctor, but it ain't no blame to this young lady. She's trying 'er 'ardest, but me leg just don't want to 'eal that's what it is."

"Well now, perhaps we might have some new ideas by this time next week. You keep it rested and I'll see what I can do."

He said no more and Camilla had not the slightest idea what he might mean. She finished the dressing a little hurriedly hoping to see him again. She wasn't disappointed; he was waiting outside.

"Are you on the verge of some new discovery?" she enquired, half humorously.

He laughed. "Unfortunately no. I intend to pick the brain of a friend of mine. I am having dinner with him

199

tomorrow evening; I was hoping you would join us?"

"At your house?" she asked, her experience of Mrs Germain's hostility and the fact that she gossiped to Miss Lees in her mind.

"No, at his," he replied solemnly, but she had seen the twinkle in his eye. She doubted he would expect her to dine alone with two batchelors. "And that of his wife, of course," he added. "They live in Park Cresent, near to Regent's Park. You are invited to dinner as my guest."

"Then thank you, I'll accept." She was sure he would hear the eagerness in her voice, and how her heart raced.

"You would prefer that I wait for you on Bloomsbury Way, no doubt?"

She agreed that she would. The girls had already had a heyday on the visits to Whitechapel.

"At seven-thirty then," he suggested. "Good day to you, Nurse Haddesley!" Then replacing his hat, he strode off in the direction of St Giles, an almost jaunty air in his walk. Camilla concluded that he was pleased with himself, but then, of course, so was she.

When she turned the corner on the following evening there was the cab waiting for her.

"A most convenient invention, the hansom cab," he observed gaily as the horse began to pull away.

"Most certainly," she agreed readily, taking the comment to be a general remark.

"No room at all for a chaperon," he continued.

She turned to look at him. "You consider then, that I need a chaperon to ride with you?" she asked him directly, remembering with amusement her conversation with Alice.

He laughed, his dark eyes shining with humour.

"Ah, what it is to have such a respectably dull reputation! One can travel with the most beautiful of women and never be suspected of anything but impeccable behaviour."

She leaned forward a little in an effort to determine the direction they were taking. Then she heard him laugh and sat back, embarrassed that he had noticed.

"Have no fear, my dear Camilla," he said gently, "we are indeed invited to dine at number twelve, Park Crescent, and our hosts are the most respectable of couples."

"Then will you not tell me their names?"

He laid his head on one side and observed her thoughtfully. "I think not," he said at last. "You do trust me," he asked suddenly, leaning a little towards her.

She did not answer straight away; she enjoyed teasing him. "Well . . ." she replied hesitantly. "Yes, I suppose I must." The laughter that burst from her lips gave her away and to her surprise he took her hand and pressed it firmly. The identity of their hosts was to be another surprise.

On their arrival a few moments later, they were shown into a well lit drawing room.

"Why, my dear James," a gentleman of around fifty said, coming towards them with a most winning smile. He was a little on the stout side, but most congenial. "And this must be Miss Haddesley. I am delighted to meet you, my dear. We've heard so much about you from James, haven't we, Agnes?" He held out his arm to a good-looking lady who came to his side, greeting James Grantly with an equal warmth. "My wife, Miss Haddesley, the greatest asset to my work that a man could have."

Agnes, Camilla could think of her as nothing more, blushed sweetly, protesting that he talked such nonsense.

Camilla glanced at James Grantly with a look that should have sent shivers down his spine. Was he to be so infuriating that he would still not tell her with whom she was to dine? The introductions had been made without the customary act of saying the hosts name.

"Joseph is so very busy," Agnes told Camilla, directing her towards a large, comfortable sofa. "He dictates his papers to me, you know. I take them down in longhand. Just roughly at first, of course. Then I copy them out later." She smiled. "I enjoy helping. His work is so interesting, you see, and so very important. Sherry, my dear?" she enquired.

Camilla accepted graciously, seething inside. She could have strangled dear James, just then. How could he leave her in such a predicament? His work was so important, Agnes was saying, and here was she agreeing, of course, without the remotest idea what his work was, apart from it being in the medical field. Joseph, he was called, but Joseph, who? Still, not a glimmer of light reached her searching brain. She glanced across at her perverse companion who was deep in conversation with their host on the other side of the room. She caught his eye and put daggered meaning into her look. This time he took the hint.

He smiled, or more precisely his mouth twisted into his lop-sided grin. "Professor Lister and I are discussing varicose ulcers," he called across, watching her face with a self-satisfied smile. "I was telling him about Mrs Gantry's leg." Leisurely he sipped from his own glass, his eyes still directed towards Camilla's.

Camilla went pale, indeed she felt quite faint which was most unusual for her. She had already expressed the silent wish to throttle James Grantly, now she would have him hung at dawn. Professor Lister! Professor Joseph Lister, the great surgeon whose lecture she had missed because of that prior engagement with Alexander. How could he? How could he have brought her to so eminent a man's house, without telling her beforehand.

"Are you ill, my dear?" Mrs Lister was saying.

Camilla turned to her swiftly, making light of her apparent indisposition. "I really am most interested in your husband's work," she said quite truthfully, but how she wished she had had the opportunity to revise her knowledge of it. She would seem quite an idiot in any conversation on the matter. And the blame would be entirely James Grantly's.

"How does your husband like working in London? It must be quite different from Edinburgh," she said, scouring her brain for the few relevant facts that were stored there.

Mrs Lister smiled, gazing into the fire for a moment. "Yes, it is, but bringing his antiseptic technique here was very important to him." She glanced at her husband for a second and smiled. "We were fortunate that they allowed us to bring four Edinburgh trained assistants with us. They were already well versed in my husband's technique." She laughed softly, shaking her head. "The staff at King's College were very suspicious at first. But they came around eventually. The results were so good, you see."

"Your husband has private patients, too, I know, Mrs Lister. My brother-in-law was fortunate to be cared for by him when he was rather badly burned."

"Ah, that would be at Fitzroy Square!"

Camilla nodded, then glanced over her shoulder at Dr Grantly. By the look of their faces they would be conversing for hours. And Camilla was ravenous.

"No idea of time at all, my dear Joseph," said his wife just as if she had read Camilla's thoughts. Then she said affectionately. "I never know when he will return from the hospital. No idea of time at all. I can have three patients awaiting him here; they could have come from anywhere in Europe especially to see him. And I know very well he has quite forgotten their appointments."

She looked over to her husband and

smiled. "Still, he'll never change now, and perhaps I wouldn't want him to. His work is the most important thing to both of us. I do all I can to help."

"I'm sure he would be lost without you," Camilla observed gently.

Agnes Lister nodded sadly. "Yes, my dear, I'm afraid he would!"

Dinner was served at last and Camilla accepted Dr Grantly's arm. "You seem to be doing admirably well with Agnes," he whispered softly in her ear.

She scowled. "I would be doing a great deal better if I had had adequate opportunity to inform myself," she retorted curtly.

He laughed. "I'm quite sure you will manage perfectly well. I thought perhaps you might be a little overawed, if I told you where we were going. As it was you were quite at ease when we arrived."

After dinner the ladies retired to the drawing room for coffee but it wasn't long before the gentleman joined them.

"We decided that as you two

ladies are so well-informed in medical matters it was unfair to exclude you from the conversation," Professor Lister announced, seating himself beside his wife.

Well informed Agnes Lister would certainly be, Camilla thought, but she herself had the horrible feeling that now she was going to fall flat on her face.

"We should like to hear all about your district nursing," the Professor continued. "Would you tell us about your work?"

Camilla breathed a sigh of relief. If there was one thing she could talk about, it was her own work. She found a captive audience who were genuinely intrigued by it all. The evening flew by and when the conversation moved to surgery she was glad to sit and listen, learning a great deal. All too soon, it seemed, it was time to leave and James Grantly was helping her on with her coat.

"You must come again," Mrs Lister invited and Camilla heard her companion

209

assuring her that they would.

"I would love to," she added, determined to speak for herself. "I really have had a most enjoyable evening."

The evening air was cold but with a rug wrapped well around her knees Camilla did not feel it. If she was truthful then she would admit that the warm glow which surged through her body was caused by the presence of the man by her side. They drove around the edge of Regent's Park; it was the longer way but she presumed the cab driver had been instructed to take that route.

"Professor Lister often takes walks in the Botanical Gardens," her companion told her. "I believe he mulls over some of his problems there."

Camilla sensed that he was looking at her in the dim light of the cab. "You enjoyed this evening," he said softly. "I'm very glad of it." It wasn't a question but more a statement of fact.

"You seemed resolved to make

things difficult for me," she retorted, determined not to let him off lightly.

"But you forgive me, don't you, Camilla?" he said in a very low voice, a voice that sent shivers down her spine.

She tried to sound angry, but the words had little passion in their ring. "I could have said the most dreadfully wrong things," she insisted.

"But you didn't, my dear Camilla. Now please, do let's forget my unforgivable neglect of your feelings, for which I do truly apologize. But you did like the Listers?"

"Very much." She held her breath.

"And you will come with me to dine with them again?"

"If you really want me to."

"Indeed, I do. Camilla, most definitely, I do." He spoke very quietly; she could barely hear the words, yet they must have been the most important words she had ever heard. And surely he must be aware of the loud thumping in her breast.

There was a silence between them for a few moments, a silence during which she felt sure they were astonishingly close in spirit. Then he spoke rather hurriedly, perhaps not wishing her to read too much into his words, or maybe, she was wrong, perhaps it was his own emotions on which he put the check.

He spoke of Professor Lister's work, but when she turned to answer him she heard the slowing of the horse's hooves and knew with regret they were almost in Bloomsbury Square. "And what about you, Dr Grantly? Would you not like to be working in the same field as Professor Lister?"

He smiled a little, nodded his head slowly. "There are times when I think myself a fool. Joseph has asked me many times to join him again. But you see, we are alike, Camilla, you and I. We see the great need of people in their own homes and we must help them." The horses had come to a standstill, but he made no move towards the door. "I wonder sometimes if it's selfishness that makes us take the hard road; a sort of self-righteous satisfaction? But no, perhaps that's unfair." He smiled at her. "I'm sure that your sense of altruism is not born of self-indulgence. You work from your heart and your patients know that you do."

"You're very hard on yourself, Dr Grantly. I doubt your motives are any different from mine."

He laughed. "What sober talk we make, and so near our parting." His voice softened. "And do please call me James when we are alone. I have already taken the liberty of using your first name, a beautiful name I must confess."

She smiled back at him. "If you wish it, and may I suggest . . . James, — " it was difficult, but how she liked saying it, — "that if I do not descend from this cab very soon, your reputation will be anything but dull. The curtains of many drawing room windows around seem to have developed a definite twitch."

He laughed again and began to open the apron doors. "Then let them talk; I do not care. I'll walk you home the rest of the way and hang my reputation. Although perhaps you may have some concern for your own?"

She shook her head. Nothing would stop her taking that walk with James Grantly tonight. "We could have met on the corner," she reminded him.

Walking beside him she knew a happiness she had never known before. They crossed the road into the central park which was clothed in shadow. He had a small lamp with him which threw a tiny glow around them.

"And by the way," he offered, halting for a moment under a vast oak tree. "If you wish to inform yourself, for the Listers' benefit, flowers and birds are Agnes' forte." He leaned a little towards her, as if to share a great secret. "She loves to talk about them. Ask her to show you her pressed flowers. Next time we dine with the Listers you will know exactly what to say."

She nodded dumbly; next time, she thought, next time. They came out through the gate on to the road again but her thoughts were interrupted abruptly by the sight of a tall, top hatted figure who was stalking up and down the pavement outside number Twenty-Three. Even in the dim light she recognised him as Alexander. What on earth had possessed him to be here at this hour of night. She glanced at her companion to see a frown on his face.

"It's Mr Buchanan," she explained, suspecting he knew this anyway. "But why he is here I cannot imagine."

Alexander, seeing them suddenly, ceased his impatient walking about and came towards them hat in hand.

"Good evening to you," he said somewhat curtly. He was obviously annoyed. "And pray what is the meaning of this summons? I have been here this last hour awaiting you."

Camilla stared at him in dismay. "Summons? But, Alexander, I have no comprehension of your meaning at all."

He glared angrily at Dr Grantly, then leaned towards Camilla with a cynical smile on his lips. "Then you will not confess to sending a cab to my house with the express message that I attend you here at once on a matter of urgency. The cab driver mistook the house, I suppose."

Camilla's face became uncomfortably red, which at once gave him the impression that she was trying to hide something. "Indeed he did, sir, for I sent no cab to fetch you, nor even thought of it."

"And I suppose he was quite deaf when he was able to repeat your name quite clearly and even describe your hair and the blue broach — the one which you wear so often."

James Grantly, feeling himself an intruder in such a personal disagreement, begged to be allowed to leave, if

Camilla was sure his presence was not required.

They bid him "Goodnight", Alexander scowling after him, and Camilla longing to follow him to reassure him that she knew nothing of this strange matter. What must he think of her?

Alexander, however, believing the doctor's presence to have been the cause of Camilla's behaviour changed his attitude at once, and putting out his hands he took both of her hands in his and held them firmly to his heart. "Camilla, dearest Camilla, now do pray admit that you sent for me and tell me what it is that caused so urgent a summons. Then I will quite forgive you for treating me so in front of that doctor fellow. You know I would come from Timbuctoo to be by your side, if you but said the word."

Camilla tried to pull away her hands, but he had them firmly by the wrists and far from letting them go he raised them to his lips and kissed her fingers one by one.

"If you do not stop it, sir, I shall raise a scream," she said. "And do stop this nonsense about my sending for you, for I did no such thing and I believe you know it."

He looked so hurt that she was at once inclined to think his story was true. She glanced rather nervously up at the windows and to her dismay saw a curtain move on the first floor. Someone was watching her. She determined at once that she must conclude this meeting as soon as possible, and make as little spectacle of it as she could.

"Alexander," she said in a calmer voice, "I do assure you that I sent no such message. I can but imagine that someone has played a trick on you. If indeed it is not you who are misleading — "

"Certainly not," he interrupted swiftly with so much conviction that she found herself believing him.

"Then I really must ask you to return home and forget all about this unpleasant incident," she told him. "I am greatly vexed that you should have been put to so much trouble for no other purpose than mischief. So I bid you good night, Mr Buchanan, and trust you will now allow me to go to my bed for I am very weary."

"No kiss for my trouble," he pleaded much to her amazement.

She slipped her hands deftly out of his and tripped swiftly up the steps to the door. "No, Mr Buchanan," she breathed in a low voice. "And good night."

At Twenty-Three Russell Square Mrs Germain had received Dr Grantly with particular pleasure. She had witnessed the meeting with Mr Buchanan and then slipped away to prepare her employer's supper time drink with special care. Upstairs in her room was a red-haired wig which she had hired from a theatrical agency for a few weeks. The brooch which she had borrowed from Camilla's room had been more difficult and its return would not be easy. Her visits to Miss Lees would supply the means but they had to be expertly timed to allow her the necessity of waiting in the house before the superintendent returned home.

9

THE next time Camilla saw James Grantly there was cholera. She had been visiting a woman whose children had rickets. She met James on the corner of Broad Street. He smiled when he saw her but she knew at once that something was wrong. His face was strained, his eyes had lost the brightness she had seen in them only the evening before. She thought at once that he had disbelieved her denial to Alexander, but he took her aside as if not wanting their conversation to be overheard.

"I have just sent two patients to the Middlesex Hospital, Camilla," he told her softly.

There was little unusual in that. She waited for the remainder of the news; she had heard more than just concern in his voice.

"It's bad, my dear, very bad. They had cholera!"

"Men?" she asked quietly. "Were they sailors?"

He shook his head; she saw the worry in his eyes, the tight muscles around his mouth. "No, both women, street women from here on Broad Street. They've admitted contact with sailors who docked over a week ago." He glanced back down the street, then put his hand gently on her arm "I'm on my way to notify the authorities, I think you should go straight away to tell Miss Lees. They've been ill for several days, my dear. There'll be more cases by tonight, many more. Tell Miss Lees to be prepared."

She whispered simply. "Yes, of course, take care, James."

Then he smiled, touched her cheek briefly before turning away and heading swiftly in the direction of Monument Street where he could get a cab.

For a moment she stood watching him walk away from her. She could never have known the change that moment would make in her life. Then, numbed and shocked by what he had told her, she began walking quickly back to Bloomsbury Square.

Miss Lees received the news with her usual calmness. "Cholera!" she said. "We must get organized at once!"

The possibility of teaching the inhabitants of those terrible dwellings in St Giles the hygienic habits that would prevent the spread of cholera would be like teaching a deaf child to hear, thought Camilla.

She did not see James to speak to for three days. There were times when she caught a glimpse of him entering some distant court, or turning a corner ahead of her. If his eyes caught hers then he would wave a hand in greeting or call across to her, but he knew she understood there was no time for thoughts of themselves. The incident of Alexander's story seemed of little importance just now.

By the fourth day patients were

being admitted to the Middlesex at the rate of twenty or so a day. The majority of these were street women from the same area as the first, but soon the disease would spread to other streets, to ordinary people, in ordinary houses, where husbands and wives and children would be writhing in pain from the cramps. The very water they needed the most was the medium that was spreading death through St Giles. Soon, the secret was out and panic seized every heart, and dread closed every door.

Hospital beds were full and more patients were nursed in their own homes. Recruitment of nurses who were to be specially trained was helpful but meant more work for those who had to train them.

For Camilla, life became a dream of work and exhausted sleep. At times sleep evaded her and she tossed and turned all night unable to leave the day behind, reliving each moment, chiding herself for some small thing forgotten.

Her hope that there might be some happiness for her with James Grantly began to fade into unreality. Then quite unexpectedly she had a message, a note in his clear hand, begging her to find time to have lunch at his house on the following day. How her heart danced that morning and how long the following one seemed.

No answer came when she lifted the knocker of Twenty-Three, Russell Square and thinking she had been too timid she banged harder. Still no sound of footsteps in the hall, still no sign of movement. She walked back to the road and looked up at the curtains, perhaps she was early. She waited, acutely embarrassed, but telling herself there were any number of reasons why neither he nor his housekeeper or maid were there to greet her. In an upstairs room Mrs Germain watched with satisfaction.

Self-consciously Camilla took out the note and read it through again. But no, there it was, clearly written, that day, that hour. She lifted the knocker once more, quite sure that the whole of Russell Square was observing her actions. After fifteen minutes she left, walking home by the shortest route and feeling thoroughly confused and quite upset.

Camilla began to think that perhaps she had imagined it all. The dinner with the Listers — was it some remarkable fantasy she had allowed herself to dream? Yet she had the note. She kept it safely, a token of reality, a proof of her own sanity.

James looked ill when she saw him at last, for there had been no further message about the luncheon. He was not ill with cholera, however, but like her, exhausted from lack of sleep. His cheeks were thinner, paler. She forgave him at once for the missed appointment.

"You received my note, Camilla?" he asked.

She nodded, trying to smile, unaware that he was referring to an apology that she had never received.

"I was so sorry to miss our luncheon. I do hope Mrs Germain looked after you."

She said: "Yes, of course." What else could she say? Had Mrs Germain therefore told him she had actually gone into the house and taken luncheon there? No, perhaps he had assumed that was what had happened.

"We are coming to the end at last," he sighed. "Another week or so and we can look for a little sunlight. I'll try to arrange to be home for lunch another day soon, and trust that another meeting won't be called to interrupt it this time."

So that was it; a meeting.

They walked together back to Bloomsbury and in the hall was a telegramme from Bernadette and Del. She read with affectionate humour, their pleas.

"*Come home to us*," they begged. "*Do not put yourself at such risk!*" The Buchanan family, they explained, had gone abroad when they had heard about the cholera. Alexander had gone with them, but had, they said, been concerned about Camilla and had asked them to persuade her to give up nursing and join them in Oxfordshire. She had not seen him for the duration of the epidemic but she did not, of course, blame him for that. She was particularly displeased however to be told there was a bouquet of flowers for her in her room. Wired from Paris, she discovered; a fact that was soon common knowledge around the home. She hoped that no one would mention them to Dr Grantly. It was hardly likely, she thought, although Miss Lees, unfortunately, never suspected Mrs Germain of ulterior motives in her interested chatter.

Jenny Hackett greeted Camilla with a warm smile when she returned to St Giles after lunch. "The doctor says things is improving," she said happily. "Ever so good 'e is. I don't know what my Alf and me would have done without 'im sometimes. We've been worried a mite about you, too, Nurse 'addesley. You look that pale these days."

"What nonsense, Jenny!" she replied, smiling. "Are we not all a little weary at this time?"

Jenny nodded and shook her head. Didn't she know it! She was glad to meet Camilla; it was a pleasant interlude after a morning of sadness. She had just left Broad Street and Mary Ware had died in her arms. She had learned to like Mary in the days she had nursed her. Even when faced with death, a warmth and humour had been Mary's. A right turn up for the book that had been. She'd never told Alf; it didn't seem right. But forgive and forget, that was her motto now.

During the next few days the Middlesex began to have empty beds. Soon Camilla knew they would begin the clearing up; the attempt to bring back to normal an area devastated by bereavement. Then once again she received a note from James; this time hurriedly scrawled.

"*Camilla, please come to luncheon today, James.*"

It was handed in at the home by a boy she did not know. She went eagerly as before, expectant, happy, and she came back miserable, disillusioned. Once again there had been no one there. Once again she had not seen the dark smiling eyes of Mrs Germain at an upstairs window.

For a week she did not see James at all; she knew from her patients that he was around but it seemed almost as if he were avoiding her. It was Alice who brought a little sunshine into her life.

"My sister's coming-out ball," she announced. "It's next week. You simply must come."

Camilla was very unsure.

Alice explained: "I've already asked Miss Lees. She's quite agreeable, in fact, she insists!"

Camilla sighed happily, then laughed. "I shall have to raid Bernadette's dressing room at Cleveland Row. I have nothing prepared for elegant balls, I'm afraid."

The evening of Katherine Kilbride's ball came and found Camilla in a most amiable mood. She had discovered a marvellous gown in pale turquoise which with her own fine jet necklace and bracelets looked quite stunning. She chose a delicate fan of cream, Nottingham lace with Mother of Pearl sticks and a hand-painted centre picture of turquoise flowers. In the mirror at Cleveland Row she felt quite excited. It was almost like her own coming-out ball all over again. Perhaps it was rebellion after so many weeks of misery. She wondered briefly if James might be there, but thought it most unlikely. She hadn't the courage to ask Alice.

The drawing rooms of Alice's home had been opened out to form a large ballroom. The walls were covered with a deep cream brocade, and the curtains at the six large, glazed doors which led to the balconies were of the same cream but embroidered with scarlet flowers.

Camilla danced a quadrille with a rather rotund gentleman who refrained from speaking except for the barest courtesies. His face remained solemn throughout the whole dance and she felt inclined to giggle whenever she glimpsed his sober countenance. The next dance was a waltz and she capered about with a short, young man who confessed quite proudly that he had never had the time to learn the steps. She refrained from telling him that he had no need to, when he could dance on other people's feet.

After this rather disappointing start, the evening improved. She had several dances with pleasant young men who were both agreeable and reasonably good at dancing. The supper, a buffet, found her being waited upon by a blond-haired man of around thirty-five who professed to being a wine merchant. He was both interesting to talk to and witty. They enjoyed a second dance, the Lancers, together.

The next waltz was, after all, a gentleman's excuse me, but she was somewhat surprised to see a hand tap on her partner's shoulder. Surprise was not the word when she saw with whom she was now dancing. James swung her around and had almost circled the floor before either of them spoke.

Then he just whispered her name, then again "Camilla!"

They danced on, spinning as if on a knife's edge, neither knowing what the other was thinking. Then he whispered again very close to her ear "I have to talk to you Camilla, I can't go on dancing like this, I have so much to explain!"

For a moment all she wanted to do was to go on forever, swirling, dancing in his arms. Then the music stopped, couples drifted off the floor. He led her to one of the comfortable couches that were set around the room. The orchestra struck up a polka but she knew it was not for her.

He was watching her face, she could

feel his eyes upon her although she kept hers on the twirling figures and the tapping feet.

"Camilla," he said softly, and she turned her eyes to his face. "You must have wondered," he began, "why I have not attempted to see you alone in the last few weeks." She tried to smile. "We have both been busy, both tired, too involved with our work" She thought about the luncheon invitations. Would she dare to ask about those?

"I could have made time, made the opportunity, you know that don't you?" He seemed almost to be begging her to criticize. She did not answer.

"I had so much to say, Camilla, so much to tell you, I had it all planned out. But then the cholera continued and I realised I had no right to speak to you as I wished. That I would have to wait to see how it ended."

She frowned, not really understanding. What was he saying? How could the progress of the cholera affect them other than at work?

But then he explained: "You see, during this epidemic I have lost all of my patients in Bloomsbury. Understandably, I suppose, they all said they could not have a physician coming into their houses who had just left a cholera bed. They gave me an ultimatum, Bloomsbury or St Giles." He shook his head. "I'm a fool, I know, but I just couldn't abandon St Giles. I thought, you see, that when it was over I could win them back. But I doubt now it will be so. Another good man has moved right in and quite honestly, Camilla, I have to consider leaving the area all together."

She touched his arm and he closed his hand over hers. "I had begun to hope, my dear, that you would be part of my future, but suddenly I have no future to offer you. Mrs Germain has stayed with me out of loyalty, pure loyalty. I have paid her no salary these last two months. I really do not know what I would have done without her."

Camilla wondered suddenly about Mrs Germain. Those notes for luncheon. The first she knew was genuine, the last? And suppose she really had told him that Camilla had lunched at his house that day! Yes, she wondered about Mrs Germain.

"My mother is widowed," he went on, "she needs my support." He stopped, lifted her chin with a crooked finger, quite oblivious for a moment that they were seated at the side of a very crowded ballroom. "Believe me, my dearest Camilla, I have nothing, absolutely nothing to offer you." He sighed deeply. "I do not even have the money to buy a practice elsewhere. And yet, for you, if it were possible, I believe I would leave St Giles."

She wanted to tell him that it did not matter, that she wanted him, not the comforts a good practice might buy. And how could she ever expect him to give up St Giles? But all around her was the tapping of dancing feet, the swish of satin and brocade, and the

236

happy, laughing chatter. She glanced around and saw Alice smiling then she knew at once, that it was she who had arranged this meeting, she, who had brought them together in this atmosphere of gaiety and romance.

"Could we talk on the terrace?" she asked. "It's too noisy here."

He hesitated, let his eyes linger a moment on hers. "Is that wise?" he asked. "It could harm your reputation, and you look so very beautiful tonight, your eyes are so blue. I swear I might kiss you if we were alone." There was a break in his voice. "And for that I have no right at all."

"Oh, hang my reputation!" she declared quite recklessly, and getting swiftly to her feet, she headed with equal speed through the terrace door.

The air was cooler outside, but she was not cold. The large pots of flowers on the balcony filled the air with their fragrance. The terrace, which she had chosen quite at random, overlooked the park. James followed her as she had known he would. In the fading light they watched the shadows of the swaying trees; saying nothing. Yet the silence was bursting with unspoken thoughts.

Chinese lanterns hung over the terrace windows, throwing a rainbow glow around.

"Miss Kilbride and her sister are very much alike," he said at last, making some attempt to begin the conversation again, but keeping his eyes firmly directed towards the park.

She clasped her hands tightly together; the resemblance between Alice and Katherine was of no interest to her at all. She said: "Yes," however, scarcely hearing her own answer. Then she turned to look up at him, detesting the etiquette that kept them apart, that prevented her from speaking out what was in her heart. How handsome he was with his black tails and white waistcoat and his dark, waving hair. It was odd, but in that strange light she could not see the tiny lines around his eyes. He looked younger, more vulnerable. A clear chiselled outline, etched against the sky. And how she loved him. Suddenly, she cared nothing for her pride.

"You consider I have no say in the matter of my own future," she said, not at all sure how to begin.

Still he kept his face averted, his hands resting on the stone wall of the terrace. "I consider your future too important to gamble with mine," he said softly. "Do you not understand, Camilla. I may have to sell up, to take a house in some quite unsuitable area. Already I have debts I cannot pay."

"And I could not be happy in a small house?" she challenged him. "You would not need a housekeeper!"

"You are used to grander houses than mine is anyway, and besides, I could not dismiss Mrs Germain, she has no other home." She heard him swallow, he almost turned his head towards her, but he forced it back, staring out now at only the blackness of the night.

Her mind raced in turmoil. Then, Del, of course, Del. He would think nothing of a few debts, an allowance even until James found his feet again. In fact he would do it gladly. "My brother-in-law," she gasped swiftly. "I'm sure he would be . . . "

She did not finish, he let out a cry like a wounded animal and stepped some paces away from her, turning his back. "Do you imagine I would even consider taking money from your family, to keep you as my wife?" he asked. "Oh Camilla, do you think so little of me as a man that you would even think of such a solution?"

She had lost; she felt nothing but defeat, then he turned around slightly, still not seeking her eyes, but looking past her as if he were afraid to meet her gaze.

"Mr Buchanan could give you a great deal more than I" he said quietly. "He would make you an excellent husband, and you will admit you like his company. You would be happier with him, much happier with him."

She swallowed hard. "Your opinion on that matter seems somewhat changeable."

He did not answer. She knew that she had to make him look at her. "James," she whispered. "I love you. Can you hear me? It's you I — "

He did not wait for her to finish, he swung around, moved towards her and stared intently down into her eyes. Then his arms went round her and his kisses burned her lips.

"You see," she gasped breathlessly when she was able. "You do care, after all."

"Of course, I care, you silly, foolish girl. I care with all my heart. But don't you see, it's quite impossible. Unless some miracle happened to change my financial position, then I shall remain as I am, extremely poor. And you, my darling, shall marry a fortune and be happy."

She pulled away from him. "Very well, James," she said, her voice wavering a little. "If that's how you want it. But first I shall wait, I shall wait for one year. If you fail to resume your former status then I shall consider myself entirely free." How hard they sounded, those words she had created for his benefit alone.

He ran his fingers across her cheek, let them linger a moment below the line of her jaw. "Would you really wait that long," he whispered, "with no guarantee of anything at the end?"

"I'd wait five times that long, James Grantly, if you wanted it," she declared vehemently.

He pulled her back into his arms. "One year, I'll agree to that, but know this, Camilla, I'm a proud man. I'll take no hand outs from your family. And I will not beg for work. I will not beg to be given some well paid post."

She lifted her face to his, her eyes dancing with pleasure. "I know that,"

242

she whispered. "I wouldn't want it any other way."

Slowly he bent to kiss her. "As I've taken the first kiss, then one more makes no matter. But that's the last, Camilla, my darling, the last time I shall ever steal your kisses when I have no right to them."

She took a cab on the following day, instructing the driver to take her to Park Crescent. There, she had a long, amicable talk with Agnes Lister, then she settled down to wait, and for the next two weeks she worked very, very hard.

A comparison of luncheon notes had revealed quite clearly that only the first was in James's handwriting, the other was forged, an outright attempt to bring discord between them. For what reason, what purpose Camilla could only guess. Mrs Germain was the obvious culprit. Camilla's original idea about Mrs Germain and James had been partly in humour. It seemed, however, to have been too near the truth. She undoubtedly hoped to keep the affection of her employer for herself? Plainly it was jealously.

Camilla found it in her heart to pity her if that were so. She was a good housekeeper, and he himself had said she was loyal. But what if that loyalty were possessive, deceitful? How far would she go? Camilla wondered? She would have to tell James, it was clear, but not whilst he was in such an unfortunate position.

The first real hope for St Giles came when Camilla had a patient ill with erysipelas who did not get cholera. So normal was this case that she found herself singing as she climbed the staircase to her next call. Life, she was sure, would soon begin to blossom; shortly she would hear from Agnes Lister.

At the top of the staircase in the dim light, she saw a man. For a moment he was so enveloped in shadow that she did not recognise him. Then as her taper lit his face, she sighed with unguarded pleasure. "Why James," she gasped, "it's you!"

Without answering he put his hand into his coat, pulled out an envelope and leaning towards her thrust it joyfully towards her hands. But before she could grasp it, a violent pain swept over her, her stomach seemed crushed in some great vice. Again the pain came and she bent forward in agony, dropping to the floor.

Then, as if in her dreams she heard the soft, deep voice. "Camilla, my darling Camilla, what is it? Tell me? What is the matter with you?"

She felt herself lifted in strong arms and then she remembered little more, and yet ... a bright light in the distance. Yes, a flickering light that grew and grew until it flamed like a furnace in the sky. She heard shouts, screams. She heard dogs barking and close to her ear a voice breathing. "Dear God, where can I take you?"

In the street, figures rushed to and fro, shouting, pointing up at the burning house and many coughing from the dense, spreading smoke. In the shadow of an archway a woman watched with satisfaction. She was about to turn away, but then she saw a tall figure emerge through the smoke with a still shape cradled in his arms. Mrs Germain stared in disbelief; she had not known that James Grantly was in the house. That the figure in his arms was Camilla she had no doubt, whether she was alive or dead, she did not know and for that information she would have to wait. She dare not stay, and she would not help him revive Camilla, anyway.

Angrily she pulled her black cloak tightly around her shoulders, hid the matches away in her bag, and then made her way discreetly along the road, not stopping until she was some distance away. As she went her mind darted in turmoil, searching, plotting, frantically seeking some other way to be rid of Camilla Haddesley once and for all.

10

CAMILLA lay quietly in her bed at Cleveland Row and watched the afternoon sunlight making patterns on the wall. Today was the first day of recovery, the first day when things were clear in her mind and Alice had just been in to visit her. The memories of the last weeks were a nightmare she wanted to forget.

That James had visited her every day she had not known until Alice's visit that day. Nor had she realised that he had carried her there to her sister's house, sending cables to Del and Bernadette, and arranging for qualified nurses from St Thomas's to attend her. What right she had to continue to live when so many had died with the same cholera she did not know, but she thanked God for it.

How she longed now to see James's face again, to watch him smile when he saw how much better she was. And surely by now he must have heard some good news from the Listers. Yes, surely they could plan their happiness now. She felt strangely, calm with an inner peace.

Then a thought occurred to her that made her pull herself up and reach for the glass on the dressing table. What a sight she must look after so long in bed! Surely her hair must need attention! What if he came this evening. The sallow skin, the sunken eyes that stared back at her were a shock, scarcely a pinkness even on her lips.

The nurse answered the bell at once. How strange, Camilla thought, that it is I who am ill, and I who must obey instructions. She was told her she must rest.

"Why, of course," she agreed readily, "but my hair, could one of the maids do my hair?"

The nurse gave in at last and Emily,

one of Bernadette's maids was sent for. Camilla did not know this nurse. She was older than she was herself and seemed very severe. At length Camilla plucked up courage to ask the question most dear to her heart.

"Has Dr Grantly been in today?" she asked with a calm voice, but racing pulse.

The nurse glanced up from the tray she was laying and frowned. "The doctor? He came this morning when you were still asleep," she announced with what Camilla felt to be an irritatingly triumphant note.

"Ah, thank you," Camilla said, hiding the wave of acute disappointment.

"First rate physician, Dr Grantly." The nurse suddenly stated at her with an air of one who knew. She was tall, heavily built and had a rather broad nose which certainly did not help her looks.

"Why, yes, indeed," Camilla replied somewhat hesitantly. She wondered on what such knowledge was based.

"I was at St Thomas's when he was a student," she was told with a purposeful emphasis on the I. "Then he came to King's College when I was working there." She shook her head and smiled to herself as if the memory pleased her. Camilla felt a surge of quite unreasonable jealousy. "I never liked his wife much. We all went to the wedding. Pretty little thing she was, I'll grant you, but altogether too fragile for a man like him. Too light-headed by half." She pounded the pillows and straightened the counterpane. "You could have knocked me down with a feather when he walked in here. I haven't seen him for . . . " She hesitated and Camilla thought she herself was going to be sick. " . . . all of two years, I should think." Then she looked her patient straight in the eye. "Mind you, he's aged, yes, I could see the difference. That wife of his most likely. And him working in St Giles, of course. I wonder what she thinks of that?"

Camilla was aware that she had gone

very white and she was glad that her being ill made it of less consequence. All she wanted to do was to get rid of that woman, get rid of everybody, to be alone in her utter, devastating misery. If she had been told she was to die the next day, she could not have been more shocked. James has a wife. James has a wife. The words kept throbbing through her head with searing agony. Why the lady was not at Bloomsbury with him she could only imagine. When at last she realised that the nurse was hurriedly taking her pulse and feeling her forehead, she forced a timid smile.

"I am rather tired," she breathed. "You were right, I should rest. No visitors tonight please. No one."

If the nurse realised that she was saying: Don't let James Grantly in, then she did not care. She did not care one jot what she thought or what she did. For in that moment Camilla hated her, hated her for destroying her life, when in all probability she had saved it by her nursing skill. If Camilla could have physically thrown her out of the room she would have done so. That there might have been some mistake, some error of recognition only came to her later and then it took her no longer than one minute to thrust the hope from her mind. James Grantly had deceived her. All those lame excuses about money. She dare not think what might have happened had she remained unenlightened. Somewhere there was a woman to whom he belonged, and yet he had allowed Camilla to believe that one day he might belong to her. Never would she forgive him . . .

★ ★ ★

At Oakland Park a month later Camilla watched the ripples on the lake as she strolled beside it. Tiny ripples scattered by the mallard and moorhens as they scuttled across the water after flies and fish. Along the bank, the willows were heavy with catkins of this, another spring.

She was well recovered, fit enough to have walked two miles from the house. But with improved health came the burden of decision, the inescapable question of whether or not she would return to nursing.

For a moment she stopped walking and let her gaze wander over the parkland. She saw the twisted shapes of ageless oaks, the slender, straight trunks of the ashes with their bright leaves and clusters of black buds. Stately chestnuts, abundant in leaf, lifted their white flower candles to the blue Maytime sky. Every where sang of springtime; every tree, every bird, every flower in the Oxfordshire countryside welcomed the warmer weather, heralding the brilliance of a summer that was to come. Yet still only misery filled Camilla's heart.

Here in the gentle countryside there were temptations to stay. Bernadette was expecting her first child in four months, and Camilla loved children dearly. Yet she did not see herself as a forever doting aunt.

She had survived cholera, but survived for what? Still, there was the emptiness, the pain. Here when the morning burst with song and colour, and the windows were thrown open to let in the clean, fresh air, there was the temptation to believe she had done enough, that it was time for others to tread the streets of London's slums, to breath the stale, odorous air of the courts.

As she turned her back on the sparkling water, she set her footsteps half-heartedly towards the house. Her hair hung loose about her shoulders; a flowered hat was in her hand, its blue silk ribbons caught around her fingers. She had always favoured blue, it went well with the copper of her hair. The watered silk dress that she wore had the blueness of the wild harebell. That day when she had looked in the glass she had been pleased, imagining herself a girl of seventeen again. But now as she strode over the springing turf she was fully aware that at twenty-five her chances of marriage were almost at an end.

Her thoughts were still far too often of James; wearisome, bitter thoughts. Yet so often she was caught unawares. When she closed her eyes she pictured him walking through St Giles, laughing beside her. In her dreams awake and sleeping she relived the things that had happened and imagined those that had not. Then reality would dawn, shame would overwhelm her, shame at her thoughts of another woman's husband.

There had been no word from him since her arrival and she was glad. After that first devastating discovery she had made it immediately became clear that he was not to be admitted to Cleveland Row. He had come time after time, she gave him credit only for persistence. Then the letters, scores of letters she had received, and returned unopened. There could be nothing he had to say.

She had a solicitor check the marriage

registers. He had traced the marriage with no difficulty at all. James Michael Grantly to Amanda Ruth Trevellion. If his wife had left him, or if indeed he had abandoned her, then it made no difference. He was still her husband and she still his wife.

Why no one in Bloomsbury had ever mentioned his wife she could not imagine. Was that perhaps the reason Mrs Germain had wished to keep them apart? But the Listers — who had known him so long — what reason could there be for their silence? At times she longed for answers, but only he could give her those, and she could not allow him to speak or write a word in his defence. She was a little afraid that if she read his letters she might be persuaded to pity him. And pity was so very close to love.

He must know she had found him out. No doubt by now, some other unsuspecting young lady was being wooed by that ruthless adventurer. How sick it made her feel to remember how gullible she had been.

After a while she reached the outer gardens which were set with orchards of plum, cherry, apple and pear. Most were bursting with blossom, spreading their pink and white petals on her hair. As she came to the formal gardens she heard the sound of a carriage rolling swiftly towards the house. Suddenly eager for company she began hurrying towards the open doors of the drawing room. But as she tripped lightly up the steps to the terrace she stopped abruptly, not daring to believe her ears.

"She is, I tell you, she's comin'. I saw 'er through that window."

Not in her wildest dreams could she have imagined hearing that voice here at Oakfield. Her heart swelling with joy she ran up the steps and burst into the drawing room.

Four pairs of arms seemed to come at her all at once, climbing up her skirt, seeking it seemed to hug her to death. Rose, Joe, Amy and Robbie dived into her outstretched arms.

When the hugging had ceased, all five were out of breath from exertion. Camilla straightened her back and sighed happily over at Bernadette. Then she saw him, the fairhaired man standing by the window. A man whom she had least expected to see. A man who had written her only formal letters since he had left London.

She stood quite speechless, surprised, confused.

"You are looking remarkably well, Camilla," he said.

She swallowed. "Thank you, I am indeed very much better." Then she glared pleadingly at Bernadette.

"Will someone not tell me what is happening? Why are the children here? And you, Alexander?"

Robbie grabbed her arm, and she noticed how he had grown although his cheeks were none the less pale and thin. She could tell that Alf and Jenny had kept a watchful eye on the children. "We've come to live 'ere, Nurse," he explained, showing concern that she did not know.

Bernadette came over swiftly and took her hands. "It's a surprise for you, Camilla darling," she explained excitedly. "You remember that the Woodfords lost all three of their children with scarlet fever last winter? Well, it occurred to Del and me that here was a mother grieving for her children and unable to have any more, whilst there in London was a small family so longing for the love of a home."

Camilla saw at once what they had done and her heart sang. She glanced at Robbie, then at Bernadette and they saw delight shining out of her eyes.

Alexander moved forward and smiled. "And I, Camilla, merely offered my services as escort; I was destined for Buchanan Hall this weekend anyway."

Camilla was still puzzled; she knew Bernadette's love of surprises, and this one had truly delighted her. But what of Alexander? It was hardly in character for him to offer to nursemaid four scruffy ragamuffins all the way from London. She found herself unreasonably distrustful of his motives.

On the way back from delivering the children she found herself alone with him. She had been so overwhelmed by news of the Gowers that her acknowledgement of Alexander's presence must have seemed remarkably casual to him. Now she remembered how long it was since they had last been together.

"Are you still angry with me, Camilla?" he asked suddenly.

She turned towards him frowning. "Angry, but why should I be angry?"

"Because I ran away when you were ill," he replied with surprising honesty.

"I am hardly likely to blame you for that."

"You are always so forgiving, Camilla, but truly I did care what happened to you. I had daily reports sent to me on your condition. Did you know that?"

The thought touched her deeply.

She wondered who it was who had sent them. "No, I didn't know," she admitted. "I assumed you wanted to forget me."

He smiled. "I did try, I'll grant you I tried, but it was quite impossible. I engrossed myself in parties, in balls, in every kind of entertainment I could find. But no, always at the back of my mind was you, Camilla. And now I see you again looking so adorably beautiful, then can you wonder why you have haunted my dreams for so long?"

He had stopped walking and turned to face her; she was quite astonished by this unexpected declaration. He took her hands in his and drew her towards him. "I have been so thoroughly miserable without you, my dearest Camilla. Indeed I can do nothing but declare my love for you and beg, yes beg that you will consider becoming my wife?"

How many times she had visualized a proposal of marriage. How many times she had dreamed of music, of flowers, of the scent of blossom as the man she loved pulled her into his arms. Yet here she was amid the fragrance of cherry blossom, with the song of the birds serenading above, and all she could do was to stare at the poor man with undisguised amazement.

"I know I don't deserve it, Camilla," he went on.

"I have treated you shockingly. I deserted you when I should have been kneeling by your bedside. But I will make it up to you, Camilla, I promise. Only say you could love me a little and I will gladly wait for an answer."

She tried to smile rather unsuccessfully. "I really do not know whether I could love you or not, Alexander. I have not seen you for some time and whilst I could not refuse you without consideration, I must entreat your patience whilst I find my feet in this sudden whirlpool. You have taken me unawares, whilst you no doubt have had a great deal of time to consider."

"But you must have known how I felt about you before your illness. I have even put the matter to my parents and obtained their approval."

"And how do they feel about having a district nurse for a daughter-in-law?"

"Why, Camilla, how you do put obstacles in the way! You are not now a district nurse, so it does not apply."

"And what if I wished to continue with that sort of work, on a voluntary basis, of course?"

His face told her the answer. She knew now the choice she had to make. She asked for two weeks to consider, to which he agreed. He also fell in with the idea that they should see as much as possible of each other during the first week, but that Camilla should have the second to herself for private thought.

She enjoyed the first week; it was a happy time. They rode a great deal and found themselves often alone, for although she had not told Bernadette, it was obvious that something was in the air. Once again she found pleasure in Alexander's company. He did everything possible to show her what a loving husband he would be.

But always in the background were Robbie and the children, now revelling in their new found home, but reminding Camilla of the people of St Giles, and of the Georgian house in Bloomsbury Square where she had found such fulfilment. Would life with Alexander be as rich, as bountiful in love, in heartbreak, and in joy? Suddenly she knew she had to see Bloomsbury again, and she had to visit St Giles.

11

SHE went to Covent Garden early
because she knew the people had
been working there since dawn.
All around her was the hustle and
bustle of a coster's day. A morning
which had begun when the donkey
carts had rattled over London's bridges,
bringing the fresh produce into this
small street market which sold fruit
and vegetables to the richest hotels
and the poorest cockney boy.

The sky was vibrant blue, a light
wind tossed the stall awnings and
rustled tissue paper around plump fruit.
Straight-backed porters passed her by,
bearing as many as seven baskets on
their heads. A hand lifted here, a nod
there, everywhere she walked there was
recognition, in every face she saw the
heart of a friend.

"Glad to see you back, Nurse

'addesley," a deep voice shouted and she turned to see Tommy Dobson smiling his broad smile, quite unaware at that moment of the empty sleeve that hung limply by his side.

"Well, if it ain't Nurse 'addesley!" another voice betrayed surprise. Bessie Lewis leaned over her well polished apples to touch Camilla's arm. She was a large woman, large in both ways, one might say, and her ample bosom at that moment threatened to crush the Granny Smiths into apple fool.

Camilla laughed. "Yes, it's me, Bessie, how are you? How's the hip these days?" she asked taking Bessie's plump hand and pressing it firmly. Bessie suffered greatly from rheumatics. She would roar with loud guffaws of laughter, however, when it was suggested that her legs would be less painful if they had less weight to carry around.

As Camilla walked on, stopping to purchase fruit, she chattered easily with the traders. Oranges from Spain, grapefruit from Cuba, her bag was soon full, but on impulse she borrowed a basket from Bessie Lewis and began filling that, too. On her departure from Oakfield Park, Del had thrust a purse in her hand. She had confessed to him about the coal and logs and he had arranged for the order to continue in her name. The purse was full of sovereigns; he had told her to enjoy herself with them.

Well, she was enjoying herself, she was spending recklessly in the market and the pleasure she would get from giving her purchases away would be ten times greater. She passed the Covent Garden Theatre and gazed up at its great stone pillars, a curious contrast, it always seemed to the market that lived so vibrantly below. Oddly enough she had never been inside it. She had attended many theatres, enjoying especially Henry Irving in his great performance of Hamlet. She had watched some marvellous portrayals by Sarah Bernhardt. Perhaps her favourites were still the Savoy Theatre productions of work by Mr Gilbert and Mr Sullivan, but nevertheless she had not had the occasion to see any of the plays at Covent Garden.

As she left the market now, laden with flowers as well as fruit, she glanced back at the colourful stalls with a peculiar nostalgia, listening to the raucous shouts and the intermittent rumbling of the donkey carts. True though it was that now this place was a busy market, once it had been the garden of a convent where the flowers and fruit had actually been grown.

"Why, Nurse 'addesley, the Lord be praised!" exclaimed Jenny Hacket when she saw Camilla standing on her freshly scrubbed, door step. "Come in, do."

Soon the kettle was hissing on the fire. "The doctor's missed you, you know," Jenny said as she took up the teapot which was warming on the hob. "I reckon the light's gone out of 'is eyes since you went away."

Camilla turned her head away.

"What nonsense, Jenny!" she said, colouring profusely.

Jenny put down the pot and laid both her hands on her hips. "You mark my words, Nurse. You two was made for each other as sure as tea is tea."

Camilla forced a laugh. "Why, Jenny," she exclaimed, "it's a proposal from another gentleman that I am considering!"

She regretted at once giving such personal information to someone so much out of her world. Yet to which world did she belong? As she had walked through the market, through Seven Dials and along the streets where she had worked so long, she felt no sense of shock, no disgust at the conditions she saw. That she would wish to improve them was obvious, but she no longer considered herself just a visitor to this area. She was a part of it, she had shared so many trials, so many joys with these people that she knew from her welcome today they considered her to be one of them;

a compliment she would not have understood a year ago when she had first stepped out of that cab into Bloomsbury Square.

"You want to wed this man, then?" Jenny asked slowly, regarding her with narrowed eyes.

Camilla fumbled in her reticule for something she did not need. "Why, as I have said, I have to consider it." It was really quite absurd to discuss her future with Jenny, however much she liked her.

"He's wealthy, this gent then?" Jenny enquired, thoughtfully stirring the tea.

Camilla nodded, remembering the time that Alexander had visited St Giles with Sir Waler. He had been sympathetic then; she thought he might be quite generous if something touched him deeply. But would that be enough? Would there not always be an ache in her heart to give of her experience, her training, to give of herself in the care of the sick? There would, she hoped, be children to care for, but would that be enough? Once made, a decision to marry Alexander would mean the end of her nursing, perhaps even the end of visits like this to these friends.

"You know the sayin', when in doubt, leave it out," Jenny said, pouring the tea. She passed Camilla a cup and sat herself at the table again. "Not that I would want to turn your mind, but we'll pray for you, Alf and I, and the Lord will show you what you do." She sipped her tea in deep thought.

Camilla was thoughtful, too. She was remembering the room to which she had gone with Miss Lees when Jenny had been so ill with peritonitis. And she recalled suddenly that it had been on that occasion that she had been introduced to James. She could still hear his voice now, commending their work in bringing the room into such good nursing order.

What a difference now! How proud Jenny was of her new home and how well kept it was. Their example and their work with the Salvation Army had a great deal of influence in St Giles.

"I have some things here for Alfred," Camilla told her quickly, deciding that the gifts she had brought would be much better dispersed by him. "And these are for you," she said laying a large bouquet of roses on Jenny's lap. "And the rest of the things, I leave it to Alfred to do as he thinks best with them."

She looked up and saw tears in Jenny's eyes. She was staring at the roses, quite unable to touch them.

"I ain't never had no flowers like this before," she whispered, "and today's our wedding anniversary, me an Alf. Been married ten years we 'ave, and the last one the best, I reckon. Thanks ever so much, Nurse 'addesley. You couldn't 'ave given me nothing better. I've always seen them roses in the market."

Camilla knew then something small she could do. She left Jenny still thanking her for 'them lovely flowers,' then returned to the market. Into her hand she counted enough sovereigns to pay for a small bunch of flowers for every week of the year, then she asked a man she trusted to deliver them to Jenny every Saturday night. She would think it extravagant, that perhaps it should have given to the 'Army', but she and Alf had brought so much light into the homes of others that she felt it a small thing to give her something that would bring some real pleasure to her own home. Perhaps, too, Camilla mused, there was a glimmer of selfishness, a thought that they would be reminded of her whatever she did in the future.

It was on the way to Bloomsbury Square that she saw the devastation. No one had mentioned it, not a word. And yet she felt it had some connection with her. The whole of one side of a court had been burned down. Nothing was left but a small piece of charred timber and a pile of blackened stones. She turned away feeling strangely sick inside. Yet why, why should she feel that this terrible sight was in any way connected with her? Hurriedly she glanced around, afraid of that hostile stone throwing crowd again. But no one was there, only a single cat, watching the stones with eager eyes, waiting, no doubt, for some incautious rat to venture abroad. Swinging around she stepped briskly towards Bloomsbury.

Only Alice was in when she knocked rather nervously on the door. Miss Lees was visiting the Paddington Home. Camilla had looked forward to seeing her again, yet perhaps she was not ready for it, Miss Lees might be overpersuasive. What she might find out about that fire razed court, frightened her even more.

Alice was very down to earth. "We're in the middle of smallpox again," she announced, as if it were a touch of gout. "Fortunately, we seem to be coming to the end of it." She looked Camilla over with deliberation. "Well, my dear, you look remarkably well. And how are things with you?"

"I am well, completely recovered, but rather indecisive."

"Indecisive about coming back?" she asked perceptively.

Camilla nodded. "I simply cannot make up my mind."

"Have you seen Dr Grantly lately?"

"Indeed I have not," Camilla barked at her rather too swiftly.

Alice laughed. "Why, how prickly you are! I merely enquired. I know you said it was over, but I did just wonder. I take it from that, you don't wish to see him. He isn't here at the moment anyway, which is perhaps fortunate."

"What do you mean, not here? You mean not in Bloomsbury?"

"No, or rather, yes, that's right! He's taken a holiday. There's another man, a Dr Stevenson from King's College, has taken over for a week or two. I don't know where James Grantly is. I could find out if you wish it?"

Camilla flushed, knowing that Alice

was watching her intently. "Whatever for?" she retorted swiftly, lowering her eyes because she hadn't the courage to meet Alice's gaze. "I have told you, we have lost all contact now. I have no wish to pursue the poor man on his holiday." She didn't add that perhaps he was taking it with his wife.

"Then you are not returning to nursing?"

She looked started. "What makes you say that?"

"Well, obviously, if you were coming back you would know perfectly well that you would have to work with him."

Camilla sighed impatiently, yet aware that this was quite unreasonable. "Coming back or not coming back has nothing to do with James Grantly. I could find work in another district, could I not?" Quickly she told Alice about Alexander, with what she considered satisfactory results. They spent the rest of the day milling it over. Alice had a day's holiday which was marvellous.

They dined together in town and walked in Regent's park afterwards. Then Alice surprised her with an invitation to a small supper party at her home. Camilla noticed that her friend seemed in a very happy mood; she seemed quite excited about the evening but would admit to no special reason. Camilla saw she would have to wait to find out why.

Another thing she waited for was the cause of that fire in St Giles. Yet that was her own doing; she put off asking about it for reasons she could not have explained. Seeing Alice again had been so pleasureable, she had drawn a veil over the fire lest it spoil the day.

It was three o'clock in the afternoon when Camilla left Alice and returned to Cleveland Row to prepare for her evening out. By four o'clock, however, she was seated in a small sitting room at the house of a Mr and Mrs Morton Craig. Camilla did not know these people nor had she, in fact, ever heard of them before she had received an invitation to take tea there from Mrs Germain who said they were her friends. The maid had obviously expected her, and had said that her host would be with her within a few minutes. Camilla watched the door with apprehension. There could be nothing gained by this meeting, yet she was curious.

The door opened and a lady in a brilliant emerald gown walked confidently into the room.

"Good afternoon, Miss Haddesley. I'm delighted you could come, and at such short notice, too." said Mrs Germain.

Camilla's first thought was how attractive the housekeeper looked. Until that moment she had always thought of her as someone dressed in muted colours and a large white apron and cap. Now, she looked brilliant, with her thick, glossy black hair and her face lightly made up; How much younger she looked!

A maid came in with tea and

they waited until she had left before speaking.

Then, "Miss Haddesley," Mrs Germain said, inclining her head and smiling, "you are wondering why I should wish to see you?" She continued, "I will be blunt. I do not like the use of euphemism, and I feel it is my duty to warn you."

Camilla allowed a brief smile to soften her face. "Then I have some idea of what it is you are to say," she told her, "but do please continue in your own way."

The girl brought in more cakes; they waited, a bursting silence between them.

"Dr Grantly," the lady began, watching Camilla's face. "James." She smiled again, lingering over his name. "A man with strange notions, my dear; one who delights in having women admire him." She raised her eyebrows. "You are not surprised?"

Camilla shook her head. "Not in the least, I know James Grantly for what he is worth, Mrs Germain. I have no illusions about him at all."

The housekeeper seemed disturbed, opening her handbag, yet seeming to find nothing in it that she required.

"Then perhaps our meeting is superfluous!" She hesitated then changed her mind all at once. "But no, I believe I should still explain." She took out her handkerchief and touched her nose lightly. "James and I," she said it slowly as if the linking of the names pleased her, "James and I, we have an understanding. For reasons I would prefer not to go into, we cannot marry."

Camilla smiled. "His wife," she said bluntly. "I know about his wife."

Mrs Germain in flushed, her hands trembled a little. "You do?" she gasped, obviously surprised. "You know about Amanda? Then my dear, you do understand!"

"Why, of course, you cannot marry, but you enjoy each other's company, shall we say, nevertheless?" How cold those words, how calm her voice, how well she hid her aching heart.

At once the surprised face broke into a warm, understanding smile. "Well, my dear, I could not have put it better myself. But as you have discovered, and I am greatly saddened that it was so, he needs to be revered by other women. He plays them along most dreadfully, but never for more than a dinner here and there, a discreet meeting alone on occasions when no doubt he tells them they are all the world to him." She shrugged. "A few kisses to keep them happy, but nothing more. And you see, my dear, he always comes back and tells me everything in the end."

This last revelation made Camilla feel quite sick, she could hardly swallow the mouthful of tea she had taken. Did this woman really know about their talks together? Did she know of his kisses on that lantern-lit terrace? How disgusting, how shocking? James Grantly became more than a deceitful man in her mind, he became the ogre she had once called him. Yet this woman loved him, she could see that quite clearly. Then she was indeed to be pitied.

Mrs Germain sighed deeply. "There have been many more like you, many of them nurses, indeed perhaps most of them nurses."

Mrs Germain laid her hand suddenly on Camilla's arm. "I was so concerned, my dear, when I realised you were becoming a victim of James's charms. You were so very vulnerable. But fortunately I was able to reprimand him long before he would have told me about your little affair." She removed her hand, took up her fan and fluttered it across her face, just once. "But then you were ill, my dear, and he did feel so dreadfully guilty I simply had to persuade him to visit you." She leaned forward a little, her eyes wide and earnest. "But it is this return to Bloomsbury now that concerns me. I know precisely what will happen when he discovers you are here. Off he will go, beginning his little flirtation all over again. And, of course, you would believe him. But you tell me, my dear, that you have already unveiled our Romeo. How glad I am that you are so sensible, so mature in your outlook." The smile again, condescending, insincere. Camilla had begun admiring her a little, now once again, she felt dislike.

Well, they were welcome to each other; they both had what they deserved. A few hours later, however, and Camilla was in for an even greater surprise.

The supper party at Alice's house had been arranged hurriedly and its purpose, the announcement of a betrothal. How Alice had managed to keep it a secret Camilla could not imagine, for the betrothal was her own. Camilla was absolutely delighted and much amused to discover that Alice's fiancé was the architect who had designed the houses for Sir Walter. How she chided her for keeping so quiet about it during the day. They had met again, it seemed quite by chance, at the house of a mutual friend and a whirlwind romance had followed. Fortunately Alice's father had approved despite the young man's lack of fortune, and Alice was madly happy.

Another unexpected happening was to involve Camilla. Alice announced that there was someone downstairs who wished to see her. She was secretive about the whole thing and would not tell Camilla who it was. Descending the stairs Camilla tossed names backwards and forwards in her mind, concluding at length that it must be Alexander; the servants at Cleveland Row where she was staying knew of her destination.

The small sitting room into which Alice showed Camilla was empty; she turned around to her friend, eyebrows raised in question.

"Go in and sit down, they are waiting in the study, I'll go and fetch them."

"They?" Camilla enquired, hearing the plural for the first time.

Alice made no reply but closed the

door behind her. Whether indeed there was more than one person Camilla doubted; it was used more likely to disguise the sex of the visitor. She became more convinced than ever that it was Alexander.

A man entered when the door was opened, a tall, dark-haired man in black tails and a white waistcoat. A man she had no wish to see at all, yet whose presence made her pulse race alarmingly. Yes, as Mrs Germain had foretold, he had come to begin his little flirtation all over again.

Calmly he placed an upturned hat on the table and laid his gloves across the top. It was a statement she did not like, a declaration that a request that he leave immediately would not be complied with. He had something to say; he intended saying it. The door closed loudly behind him.

She felt the colour drain from her cheeks, and then it rose again as sudden anger took over her mind. How could she, how could Alice have allowed this man, this deceitful man into her house? But then she remembered, she had never told Alice that James Grantly was married. She had never revealed the reason for her apparently sudden change of heart.

"I see I am still not welcome, Miss Haddesley," he said, his voice so low that it was almost a whisper. His dark eyes swiftly scanned her person from her satin shoes to her up swept hair.

Swiftly she got to her feet, swung around and turning her back on him, walked to the fireplace. Then she worked her fan rapidly and stared into the flickering flames. "Indeed, sir, you are not," she replied, managing to keep her voice quite calm.

"Then, I can only beg that you tell me why. I have written some twenty times to ask you, but my letters were returned unopened. That I have offended you is obvious, but how? I beg you to tell me that I may at least know what is my crime."

He moved towards her, his hands

outstretched and when she turned her head to look at him there was so much pain on his face that she dare not look again. How easy it would be to forgive him! How easy to believe any fabricated story he cared to concoct. And how nearly he convinced her that he did not know the reason for her displeasure. She told herself firmly all of three times, he is married to another woman . . . he is married to another woman, and he has made a mistress of yet another. In coming here he not only deceives me but them also. Then she swung round to face him, her head held high, her eyes averted to reach only his necktie because she dare not look into his anguished eyes.

"You dare to ask what you have done?" she demanded. "You dare to come here, pleading ignorance of your crime. How could you use my friend for such deceit? Go away, get out of here! I never, never wish to see you again."

His hands came out towards her as

if they would grasp her and shake her like a child. She stepped aside but he came on and held her firmly by the arm. "For pity's sake tell me, Camilla." His voice was raised now, almost to a shout. "Camilla, I love you, I have a post at Great Ormond Street Hospital, I can support you, I need you so."

She paid no heed at all to his words; she knew about the post. She did not bother to tell him that it was she who had asked the Listers to arrange it. She pulled away from his hands and threw him a look which she hoped would still his tongue. Then she marched to the door.

"Camilla," he cried, "tell me, is it the fire, is it the fire?"

She slammed the door behind her and stormed up the stairs. In Alice's room which had been put at her disposal she flung herself on to the bed and sobbed until her head ached and her eyes were swollen and red.

It was Alice's voice which she heard

at last calling her name, and she sat up and took a handkerchief to wipe the tears from her face.

"Camilla, oh, Camilla darling, what have I done? For goodness' sake, tell me. I thought you ought to see him before you decided about Alexander. I sent for him, yes I sent a cable to Portsmouth where he was staying with his mother."

"How do you know it was his mother?" Camilla demanded with quite unreasonable anger.

She looked shocked, not understanding the line of thought. "Why, Mrs Germain told Miss Lees it was so," she said. "She said he often goes to visit her."

Camilla blew her nose loudly. "Well, it's probably his wife," she said, hiccoughing from the sobbing.

"His wife! Don't be silly, he hasn't got one!"

Camilla took a deep breath. "Oh yes, he has," she shouted, sounding like a spoilt child. "The nurse at Cleveland Row told me. She went to his wedding, and I've seen a copy of the marriage certificate."

Alice said nothing. She sat down on the bed as stunned as Camilla had meant her to be. Then she sighed, a great heaving sigh. "I see now," she admitted, "I understand why you wouldn't see him. But why, oh why, didn't you tell me, Camilla? I would never have done such a thing had I known!"

Camilla found it hard to explain why she hadn't told Alice before; she was ashamed really of having been taken in by a man so she had tried to hide it.

"How could he?" Alice kept saying. "How could he?"

Camilla felt better now, sharing the knowledge had somehow made it easier to bear. She told her about her tea with Mrs Germain. Then, "Tell me about the fire, Alice," she demanded, remembering his parting words.

Alice was at once disturbed by the question. Her eyes darted nervously around the room, as if searching for escape. Camilla prepared herself for something unpleasant, she was too obviously reluctant to enlighten her.

"Well, how much do you remember, Camilla?" she asked at last.

Camilla frowned. "Remember, what of exactly?"

"Why the fire. Do you remember it at all?"

She searched her brain, but nothing came to her mind but the picture of devastation she had seen today.

She shook her head.

"The day you became ill, when . . . " Alice hesitated, "when he . . . took you to Cleveland Row. You were in one of those courts. Don't you remember that? You collapsed and he carried you out of the house."

A picture formed in her mind, James at the top of the stairs leaning down towards her; then the pain, then the feeling of being carried, then . . . She sat up suddenly, the bright light . . . the noise . . . yes, now she remembered, A fire, that's what it was, fire! But still the images were not clear. "But how?" she asked quietly.

Alice looked distressed again, then she swallowed hard. "They thought . . . that perhaps you dropped your taper, Camilla," she said, her voice barely more than a whisper.

"My taper? They . . . who are they?"

"The authorities. You know they have to investigate these things. They decided that you weren't at all to blame. I mean Dr Grantly told them quite clearly that you collapsed, you were unconscious when he carried you out of the house. In fact, they said that if anything, he was more to blame for not seeing you had dropped it and stamping out the flame. But it went no further. They said they understood that he was concerned about you and they brought in a verdict of accidental death."

Camilla stared at her. "Death, whose death?"

"Why . . . the three people who died in the fire. They were trapped, you

292

see. The flames spread so rapidly. You know what those houses are like. It wasn't your fault at all. They said that in court. They said it was the condition of the houses, the wood in them being so rotten, and it was the stairs collapsing that trapped them, you see."

Camilla put her hands over her eyes. She had escaped down those stairs, James Grantly, too. How close had they been to death? And how could she ever forget, whatever the court might have said, that it had been her taper that had started the fire? She felt sick with guilt. Her personal grief about love had no importance anymore. Once again she began sobbing and this time it was for St Giles.

The fire, it transpired, had done one good thing — it had brought to the attention of the authorities the condition of the houses. Yet again they were reminded, Camilla's many letters to them were apparently read out in court. Plans had been drawn up for redevelopment of that whole street; the houses that Sir Walter had built were taken as an example and she was to see the whole area rebuilt. The architect, quite naturally was Alice's husband.

★ ★ ★

Camilla arrived back at Oakland Park on the following evening. Bernadette must have sensed her downcast mood because she did not question her about London which was unusual. Alexander had gone to Reading on business for the estate, so he would not be back until Thursday. She was relieved; it would give her time to compose herself in readiness to give him his answer.

On the Thursday morning she put on her blue watered silk dress, the one she had been wearing when he had proposed to her, then she went for along, long walk. It was a beautiful day, the sun was wonderfully warm and a score of butterflies flitted around the flower garden as she wandered through. She enjoyed the walk; she felt calmer now. In the beech wood she was surprised to meet Robbie. He grinned cheekily at her.

"Why are you not at school?" she asked.

"Got an 'eadache," he replied, still grinning. "Ma Woodford said I needn't go today. She said to go for a walk to see if it went off."

She gathered from his smiling face that the cure had worked.

"Bin looking for you," he said suddenly. "I got somethin' for you." He held out a piece of paper which was somewhat crushed in his hot hand.

She took the paper and opened it. A second sheet was inside.

"'e said to tell you she died, and to read 'em both."

What a strange message! She looked up. "Who said?" she demanded swiftly.

"The doctor; he said you was to read it 'cause it would show it was true."

She tore open the paper and read the heading at the top of the page.

It was a death certificate, and as she read the names below tears ran down her cheeks. '*Amanda Ruth Grantly,*' she read, '*Wife of Dr James Michael Grantly, died this . . .*' Her finger raced to the year: '*1877*', almost two years ago since his wife had died of consumption. For a moment she stared at Robbie, then she read the second paper. '*Miss Haddesley, Everything I told you was untrue. Phillida Germain.*'

She looked at Robbie again, then she grabbed him by the shoulders. "Where is he?" she shouted. "When did he give you these?"

He shook himself free. "Over there in the garden. I come straight away, but I told you I've been looking for you. And Nurse, he said . . ."

"Yes," she called back.

"'e said if you wanted 'im, 'e'd be by the fountain."

She was gone almost before he had finished. Across the park, through the orchards and under the great yew arch.

Then she stopped, straightened her hair, and smoothed down her dress before walking in a most ladylike manner up the path to the fountain.

He was there, standing with his back to her; and she was glad he did not see her approach. She said his name softly and he spun around. She held out the papers towards him. "Robbie," she whispered, "he gave me these. Oh James, I'm so sorry, I didn't know."

He took the papers without looking at them and thrust them into his coat pocket. She saw how pale he was, how dark around the eyes. Yet still handsome, still making her heart thud in her breast. And in those dark eyes still the doubts.

She smiled and held out her hands to him, words failing when she needed them most.

He gripped her hands in his and she saw the joy that leapt into his eyes. Then all at once she was in his arms. He kissed her hair, her cheek, her lips.

When he released her she was quite out of breath. "When in doubt," Jenny had said. She had no doubts now about James Grantly. She knew she loved him, and now she knew he had the right to love her.

"Camilla, darling Camilla," he whispered, "there's so much to say, so much to explain. I hardly know where to begin."

"Would you tell me about your wife, James? Could you start at the beginning?" She realised it might be painful for him, but it seemed best to talk about it now, to get the shadows away and fill them with light. He nodded, then looking around he sat down on the edge of the fountain and pulled her on to his knee.

"Her name was Amanda," he began, "she was very beautiful and I loved her, Camilla. I loved her very much. But I knew before we married that she had not many years to live. She knew nothing of this, she thought our lives together would be long and happy. But

I . . . I knew they would be short, and I did my best to make them good. She was very different from you, Camilla. Rather frivolous in many ways; I doubt she would have liked the life I lead now. St Giles would have meant nothing to her, indeed I think it unlikely she would have been happy at Russell Square. She died eighteen months after our marriage, shorter than I had hoped, and I confess I missed her no less for knowing it would happen. She was Mrs Germain's sister, Camilla. When Albert Germain died, he was thirty years older than she, he left all his fortune to his mistress. I felt it my duty to give her a home. It seems she has repaid me badly. She has been a good housekeeper, but oh, my darling, what has she done to you? Yet it was she herself who enlightened me."

He smiled. "She apparently had designs on me herself, although, goodness knows why, I could never have married her; she was my sister-in-law! We had a slight disagreement and she actually broke down and said that I didn't know how grateful I should be to her. I thought, of course, she was referring to her house-keeping but she mentioned your name, and well, you can imagine, I demanded that she explain what she was talking about. Then it all came out; the terrible things she had done." He spoke quietly now, deeply moved by his own words. "The fire — did you know she started that fire?"

Camilla shook her head.

He went on: "But now, I thank God I know why you thought so badly of me. She told me you knew I had been married and I realised at once that you thought I had a wife still living. How I blamed myself for not telling you earlier! Oh, Camilla, if only you knew how I longed to talk to you when you were well again. They had offered me this part-time post at Great Ormond Street Hospital. I realised when you were ill what a fool I had been to give you up so easily. Joseph Lister would have found me a post if only I had asked."

Camilla dropped her eyes and hoped he didn't notice the smile on her lips.

He shook his head again. "I still can't believe this is real, that the nightmare of so many months in over."

She lifted her face to his again. "Oh, James, how sorry I am that I have treated you so badly." She was filled with remorse. How cruel she had been! She sighed.

"What sorrow we cause ourselves when we do not put our thoughts into words. If only I had told you!"

He laughed; his eyes suddenly bright with joy. "Then I must put voice to my thoughts this minute. Will you come back to Bloomsbury, my darling Camilla, will you come back as my wife?"

She did not remember answering because she was suddenly aware of being very, very wet. "It's raining," he exclaimed laughing and getting to his feet.

Camilla looked up at the sky. "It is not," she disagreed emphatically. "Someone has turned on the fountain!"

A small face peeped out from the roses, a cheeky grin spreading from ear to ear.

"You just come here, Robbie Gower," she called, and he came over, hands in pockets, shuffling his feet, but with a surprising twinkle in his eye.

"Mr Alexander was looking for you, Nurse," he said quite confidently.

She felt James stiffen, his hand closed tighter over hers.

"It's all right, Nurse," Robbie went on, rubbing his ear. "I told him I thought you was down by the water. I mean, I didn't actually say the lake, but I didn't say the fountain neiver."

How they laughed! Even the thought of poor Alexander tramping two miles to the lake for nothing could not mar their happiness. She looked up at James and his eyes laughed down into hers. Then he took her in his arms and quite disregarding young Robbie who stood there grinning beside them, he kissed her again, and again . . . and again!

THE END

WITH SOMEBODY ELSE
Theresa Charles

Rosamond sets off for Cornwall with Hugo to meet his family, blissfully unaware of the shocks in store for her.

A SUMMER FOR STRANGERS
Claire Hamilton

Because she had lost her job, her flat and she had no money, Tabitha agreed to pose as Adam's future wife although she believed the scheme to be deceitful and cruel.

VILLA OF SINGING WATER
Angela Petron

The disquieting incidents that occurred at the Vatican and the Colosseum did not trouble Jan at first, but then they became increasingly unpleasant and alarming.

DOCTOR NAPIER'S NURSE
Pauline Ash

When cousins Midge and Derry are entered as probationer nurses on the same day but at different hospitals they agree to exchange identities.

A GIRL LIKE JULIE
Louise Ellis

Caroline absolutely adored Hugh Barrington, but then Julie Crane came into their lives. Julie was the kind of girl who attracts men without even trying.

COUNTRY DOCTOR
Paula Lindsay

When Evan Richmond bought a practice in a remote country village he did not realise that a casual encounter would lead to the loss of his heart.

ENCORE
Helga Moray

Craig and Janet realise that their true happiness lies with each other, but it is only under traumatic circumstances that they can be reunited.

NICOLETTE
Ivy Preston

When Grant Alston came back into her life, Nicolette was faced with a dilemma. Should she follow the path of duty or the path of love?

THE GOLDEN PUMA
Margaret Way

Catherine's time was spent looking after her father's Queensland farm. But what life was there without David, who wasn't interested in her?

HOSPITAL BY THE LAKE
Anne Durham

Nurse Marguerite Ingleby was always ready to become personally involved with her patients, to the despair of Brian Field, the Senior Surgical Registrar, who loved her.

VALLEY OF CONFLICT
David Farrell

Isolated in a hostel in the French Alps, Ann Russell sees her fiancé being seduced by a young girl. Then comes the avalanche that imperils their lives.

NURSE'S CHOICE
Peggy Gaddis

A proposal of marriage from the incredibly handsome and wealthy Reagan was enough to upset any girl — and Brooke Martin was no exception.

A DANGEROUS MAN
Anne Goring

Photographer Polly Burton was on safari in Mombasa when she met enigmatic Leon Hammond. But unpredictability was the name of the game where Leon was concerned.

PRECIOUS INHERITANCE
Joan Moules

Karen's new life working for an authoress took her from Sussex to a foreign airstrip and a kidnapping; to a real life adventure as gripping as any in the books she typed.

VISION OF LOVE
Grace Richmond

When Kathy takes over the rundown country kennels she finds Alec Stinton, a local vet, very helpful. But their friendship arouses bitter jealousy and a tragedy seems inevitable.

CRUSADING NURSE
Jane Converse

It was handsome Dr. Corbett who opened Nurse Susan Leighton's eyes and who set her off on a lonely crusade against some powerful enemies and a shattering struggle against the man she loved.

WILD ENCHANTMENT
Christina Green

Rowan's agreeable new boss had a dream of creating a famous perfume using her precious Silverstar, but Rowan's plans were very different.

DESERT ROMANCE
Irene Ord

Sally agrees to take her sister Pam's place as La Chartreuse the dancer, but she finds out there is more to it than dyeing her hair red and looking like her sister.

HEART OF ICE
Marie Sidney

How was January to know that not only would the warmth of the Swiss people thaw out her frozen heart, but that she too would play her part in helping someone to live again?

LUCKY IN LOVE
Margaret Wood

Companion-secretary to wealthy gambler Laura Duxford, who lived in Monaco, seemed to Melanie a fabulous job. Especially as Melanie had already lost her heart to Laura's son, Julian.

NURSE TO PRINCESS JASMINE
Lilian Woodward

Nick's surgeon brother, Tom, performs an operation on an Arabian princess, and she invites Tom, Nick and his fiancé to Omander, where a web of deceit and intrigue closes about them.

THE WAYWARD HEART
Eileen Barry

Disaster-prone Katherine's nickname was "Kate Calamity", but her boss went too far with an outrageous proposal, which because of her latest disaster, she could not refuse.

FOUR WEEKS IN WINTER
Jane Donnelly

Tessa wasn't looking forward to meeting Paul Mellor again — she had made a fool of herself over him once before. But was Orme Jared's solution to her problem likely to be the right one?

SURGERY BY THE SEA
Sheila Douglas

Medical student Meg hadn't really wanted to go and work with a G.P. on the Welsh coast although the job had its compensations. But Owen Roberts was certainly not one of them!

HEAVEN IS HIGH
Anne Hampson

The new heir to the Manor of Marbeck had been found. But it was rather unfortunate that when he arrived unexpectedly he found an uninvited guest, complete with stetson and high boots.

LOVE WILL COME
Sarah Devon

June Baker's boss was not really her idea of her ideal man, but when she went from third typist to boss's secretary overnight she began to change her mind.

ESCAPE TO ROMANCE
Kay Winchester

Oliver and Jean first met on Swale Island. They were both trying to begin their lives afresh, but neither had bargained for complications from the past.

CASTLE IN THE SUN
Cora Mayne

Emma's invalid sister, Kym, needed a warm climate, and Emma jumped at the chance of a job on a Mediterranean island. But Emma soon finds that intrigues and hazards lurk on the sunlit isle.

BEWARE OF LOVE
Kay Winchester

Carol Brampton resumes her nursing career when her family is killed in a car accident. With Dr. Patrick Farrell she begins to pick up the pieces of her life, but is bitterly hurt when insinuations are made about her to Patrick.

DARLING REBEL
Sarah Devon

When Jason Farradale's secretary met with an accident, her glamorous stand-in was quite unable to deal with one problem in particular.